Grammar & Writing Practice

Let's See Grammar

Reflexive pronouns
反身代名詞

lick itself

Basic 2

彩圖初級英文文法 三版

written by Alex Rath Ph.D.

Expressions without "the"
不加the的情況

coffee

Uncountable nouns
不可數名詞

cheese

Counting an uncountable noun
不可數名詞的計算

a box of chocolate

Countable nouns
可數名詞

have the breakfast

some apples

Basic 2 Contents

Let's See Grammar

Basic 2

彩圖初級英文文法　三版

Answers to Small Exercises

p. 8 1. wants to buy 2. hopes to learn

p. 14 1. to buy 2. to tell 3. for the exam 4. for the new toy

p. 48 1. Would you like 2. Would you like to go 3. Would you like me to open 4. Shall I draw

p. 50 1. What shall we do 2. How about going to

p. 86 1. nice 2. happy 3. is tall 4. smells good

Answers to Practice Questions

Unit 50   p. 9

1 1. watch 2. to play 3. fly 4. to give 5. going / to go 6. to win 7. hear 8. play 9. go 10. to be 11. to meet
2 1. to pay the bill
   2. to quit drinking and smoking
   3. make good coffee
   4. look very happy; to wear clothes
   5. to work 10 hours a day
   6. to buy some red peppers

Unit 51   p. 11

1 1. to finish 2. go 3. sit 4. to fly 5. to join 6. to call 7. to call 8. make / to make 9. to have 10. to throw 11. to sit
2 1. to get the sausage on the plate
   2. take a look at your answers
   3. to climb a tree
   4. to eat on a train
   5. to bake cookies
   6. to study for the exam
   7. to read a story to you
   8. to finish the paper today

Unit 52   p. 13

1 1. playing soccer 2. making clothes
   3. blowing bubbles 4. singing a song
   5. drawing on canvas 6. biking
   7. waiting for his master
   8. walking in the rain
2 1. call / to call 2. to avoid 3. drinking
   4. getting up / to get up 5. swimming
   6. sharing 7. going 8. living 9. running
   10. going / to go 11. meeting 12. eating

Unit 53   p. 15

1 1. a library to borrow books
   2. a history museum to see artifacts
   3. the aquarium to see the fish
   4. an art gallery to look at paintings
   5. the amusement park for fun
   6. a zoo to see the animals
2 1. for carrying liquid cement
   2. for putting out fires
   3. for towing cars and trucks
   4. for taking the sick or wounded to the hospital
   5. for pushing soil and rocks

Unit 54 Review Test   p. 16

1 1. surf 2. to surf 3. surfing / to surf, surfing 4. ski 5. to ski 6. skiing 7. drive 8. drive / to drive 9. driving 10. to drive
2 1. My parents went out for a walk.
   2. Mr. Lyle went to the front desk for his package.
   3. I have to get everything ready for the meeting.
   4. I jog every day to stay healthy.
   5. I walked into the McDonald's on Tenth Street to buy two cheeseburgers.
3 1. C 2. A 3. B 4. A 5. C 6. B 7. C 8. B 9. C 10. B 11. B 12. B 13. B 14. B 15. C
4 1. the beach to play beach volleyball
   2. the water to get the ball
   3. the supermarket for some milk
   4. the opera house for a concert
   5. the store to buy a gift
   6. my friend's house to see her new doll house
   7. the dentist's for a dental checkup
   8. the Starbucks for a cup of latté
   9. the stadium to watch a baseball game
   10. the market to buy some pumpkins
5 1. ✓ 2. ✗ I should visit my sister.
   3. ✗ Let's go to see a movie. 4. ✓
   5. ✓ 6. ✗ I want you to call me next week.
   7. ✗ Would you like me to call you next week?
   8. ✓ 9. ✗ When you finish playing cards, call me.
   10. ✗ I go swimming every morning at 6:00.
   11. ✓
   12. ✗ Most people love to go on a vacation. / Most people love going on a vacation.
   13. ✓
   14. ✗ Kelly went to see the doctor to have a checkup.
   15. ✓

Unit 55   p. 21

1 1. go bowling   2. go swimming   3. go skiing
     4. go sailing   5. go camping   6. go skating
2 1. has gone   2. go for   3. have gone by
     4. going   5. going for   6. went on   7. went

Unit 56   p. 23

1 1. to finish   2. to listen   3. to fix   4. done
     5. cut   6. washed
2 a shower, a walk, a nap, a look, a note, a
     picture, a shortcut, a chance, a seat
3 1. Get on, get off   2. took   3. get over
     4. Take off   5. take part in
     6. gotten together   7. of

Unit 57   p. 25

1 1. a favor   2. a mistake   3. good   4. his best
     5. a wish   6. a speech   7. the decision
2 1. do   2. make   3. made   4. do   5. made of
     6. made from   7. good   8. made of   9. fly
     10. sad

Unit 58   p. 27

1 1. He had the pants shortened.
     2. Yvonne had her son mop the floor.
     3. She had the car washed.
     4. She had her husband replace the lightbulb.
     5. He had the paper folded.
     6. She had the box packed with books and
         sent to the professor.
     7. He had his students read thirty pages of
         the book a day.
     8. I'm going to have this gift wrapped.
2 1. have your baby
     2. have something to do with
     3. has nothing to do with
     4. have a look
     5. have a good time
     6. having a haircut

Unit 59 Review Test   p. 28

1 1. A   2. C   3. A   4. B   5. A   6. B   7. B   8. C
     9. C   10. A   11. C   12. C   13. A   14. C
2 1. is made from   2. went for   3. get along
     4. took part in   5. go on   6. took place
     7. Get over   8. is made of
3 1. finish   2. to change   3. finished   4. clean
     5. apologize   6. work   7. done   8. painted
     9. to remove   10. explain   11. repaired
4 1. Did you **have** your hair cut last week?
     → **Yes, I did. I had my hair cut last week.
     / No, I didn't. I didn't have my hair cut
     last week.**

     2. Do you have to **do** a lot of homework
         tonight?
     → **Yes, I do. I have to do a lot of homework
     tonight. / No, I don't. I don't have to do
     a lot of homework tonight.**
     3. Does your family **go** on a picnic every
         weekend?
     → **Yes, we do. We go on a picnic every
     weekend. / No, we don't. We don't go
     on a picnic every weekend.**
     4. Do you like to **take** pictures of dogs and
         cats?
     → **Yes, I do. I like to take pictures of dogs
     and cats. / No, I don't. I don't like to
     take pictures of dogs and cats.**
     5. Do you **take** care of your little sister when
         your parents are out?
     → **Yes, I do. I take care of my little sister
     when my parents are out. / No, I don't.
     I don't take care of my little sister when
     my parents are out.**
     6. Do you like to **go** camping on your
         summer vacation?
     → **Yes, I do. I like to go camping on my
     summer vacation. / No, I don't. I don't
     like to go camping on my summer
     vacation.**
     7. Do you **do** the dishes every day?
     → **Yes, I do. I do the dishes every day. /
     No, I don't. I don't do the dishes every
     day.**
     8. Do you **take** a shower in the morning?
     → **Yes, I do. I take a shower in the
     morning. / No, I don't. I don't take a
     shower in the morning.**
     9. Do you **go** crazy with your homework
         every day?
     → **Yes, I do. I go crazy with my homework
     every day. / No, I don't. I don't go crazy
     with my homework every day.**
     10. Do you **make** a lot of mistakes?
     → **Yes, I do. I make a lot of mistakes. / No,
     I don't. I don't make a lot of mistakes.**
     11. Have you ever **had** the dentist fill a cavity?
     → **Yes, I have. I have had the dentist fill a
     cavity. / No, I haven't. I haven't had the
     dentist fill a cavity.**
5 **do:** exercise, the laundry, the shopping
     take: a nap, a bath, a break
     make: friends, a wish, money

Unit 60   p. 33

1 1. Chris can play the guitar.
     2. Chris can't play the drums.
     3. Chris can't play the piano.

3

4. Chris can play the flute.

5. Chris can play the violin.

6. Chris can't play the saxophone.

2 1. Yes, I can. I can speak English.
/ No, I can't. I can't speak English.

2. Yes, I can. I can read German.
/ No, I can't. I can't read German.

3. Yes, I can. I can hang out with my friends on the weekend. / No, I can't. I can't hang out with my friends on the weekend.

4. Yes, I can. I can run very fast.
/ No, I can't. I can't run very fast.

5. Yes, she can. She can cook Mexican food.
/ No, she can't. She can't cook Mexican food.

6. No, it can't. A dog can't fly.

7. No, it can't. A pig can't climb a tree.

8. No, we can't. We can't speak loudly in the museum.

Unit 61 p. 35

1 1. could paint pictures

2. could write calligraphy

3. could sculpt figures

4. could shoot photographs

5. could make pots

6. could paint landscapes

2 1. Yes, I could. I could play the piano when I was twelve. / No, I couldn't. I couldn't play the piano when I was twelve.

2. Yes, I could. I could swim when I was twelve. / No, I couldn't. I couldn't swim when I was twelve.

3. Yes, I could. I could use a computer when I was twelve. / No, I couldn't. I couldn't use a computer when I was twelve.

4. Yes, I could. I could read novels in English when I was twelve. / No, I couldn't. I couldn't read novels in English when I was twelve.

5. Yes, I could. I could ride a bicycle when I was twelve. / No, I couldn't. I couldn't ride a bicycle when I was twelve.

Unit 62 p. 37

1 1. must finish   2. mustn't smoke

3. had to clean   4. mustn't fight

5. must come   6. must finish

7. had to break   8. mustn't eat

9. must behave   10. had to run

2 1. You must hurry.

2. You must go to bed.

3. You must eat something.

4. You must drink something.

5. You must be careful.

6. You mustn't fight with them.

7. You mustn't lose it.

Unit 63 p. 39

1 1. She has to pack products.

2. She has to work on the computer.

3. She has to answer the phone.

4. She has to make copies.

2 1. doesn't have to deliver the mail.

2. don't have to make coffee.

3. doesn't have to show up every day.

4. doesn't have to fax documents.

Unit 64 p. 41

1 （答案略）

2 1. You mustn't smoke

2. You don't have to pay cash

3. You mustn't skateboard

4. You mustn't talk on a cell phone

5. You don't have to pay full price

Unit 65 p. 43

1 1. may/might block the shot

2. may/might hit a home run

3. may/might win the set

4. may/might score a touchdown

5. may/might win the race

6. may/might clear the bar

2 1. We may go to the seashore tomorrow.

2. I might take you on a trip to visit my hometown.

3. We may pick up Grandpa on the way.

4. We might visit my sister in Sydney next year.

5. My sister may bring her husband and baby to visit us instead.

6. We might go to Hong Kong for the weekend.

7. You may go to a boarding school in Switzerland.

8. Or you might go to live with your grandparents.

Unit 66 p. 45

1 1. shouldn't eat   2. should yield

3. shouldn't cheat   4. should respect

5. shouldn't arrive   6. should work

7. shouldn't feed   8. should take

2 1. →Should I call the director about the resume I sent?

→Do you think I should call the director about the resume I sent?

2. →Should I bring a gift with me?
   →Do you think I should bring a gift with me?
3. →Should Mike go on a vacation once in a while?
   →Do you think Mike should go on a vacation once in a while?
4. →Should we visit our grandma more often?
   →Do you think we should visit our grandma more often?
5. →Should I ask Nancy out for a date?
   →Do you think I should ask Nancy out for a date?
6. →Should Sally apply for that job in the restaurant?
   →Do you think Sally should apply for that job in the restaurant?

Unit 67   p. 47

1 1. →May I get two more shirts just like this one?
   →Could I get two more shirts just like this one?
   →Can I get two more shirts just like this one?
2. →May I have three pairs of socks similar to these?
   →Could I have three pairs of socks similar to these?
   →Can I have three pairs of socks similar to these?
3. →May I have a tie that goes with my shirt?
   →Could I have a tie that goes with my shirt?
   →Can I have a tie that goes with my shirt?
4. →May I pay with a credit card?
   →Could I pay with a credit card?
   →Can I pay with a credit card?
2 1. May I speak to Dennis?
2. May I borrow your father's drill?
3. Could you move these boxes for me?
4. Could you turn up the heat?
5. Can I put my files here?

Unit 68   p. 49

1 1. →Would you like some fruit salad?
   →Would you like me to make some fruit salad?
   →I'll make some fruit salad for you.
     Shall I make some fruit salad for you?
2. →Would you like some tea?
   →Would you like me to make some tea?
   →I'll make some tea for you.
   →Shall I make some tea for you?

3. →Would you like some orange juice?
   →Would you like me to squeeze some orange juice?
   →I'll squeeze some orange juice for you.
   →Shall I squeeze some orange juice for you?
4. →Would you like some pudding?
   →Would you like me to make some pudding?
   →I'll make some pudding for you.
   →Shall I make some pudding for you?
2 1. Would you like to go fishing
2. Would you like to play basketball
3. Would you like to go hiking
4. Would you like to go to the beach
5. Would you like to have some pizza

Unit 69   p. 51

1 1. →Shall we play another volleyball game?
   →Why don't we play another volleyball game?
   →How about playing another volleyball game?
   →Let's play another volleyball game.
2. →Shall we go on a picnic?
   →Why don't we go on a picnic?
   →How about going on a picnic?
   →Let's go on a picnic.
3. →Shall we eat out tonight?
   →Why don't we eat out tonight?
   →How about eating out tonight?
   →Let's eat out tonight.
4. →Shall we take a walk?
   →Why don't we take a walk?
   →How about taking a walk?
   →Let's take a walk.
5. →Shall we go to Bali this summer?
   →Why don't we go to Bali this summer?
   →How about going to Bali this summer?
   →Let's go to Bali this summer.
6. →Shall we have Chinese food for dinner?
   →Why don't we have Chinese food for dinner?
   →How about having Chinese food for dinner?
   →Let's have Chinese food for dinner.

Unit 70 Review Test   p. 52

1 1. Q: Can you boil tea eggs?
   A: Yes, I can. I can boil tea eggs. / No, I can't. I can't boil tea eggs.
2. Q: Can you purée tomatoes?
   A: Yes, I can. I can purée tomatoes. / No, I can't. I can't purée tomatoes.
3. Q: Can you deep fry French fries?
   A: Yes, I can. I can deep fry French fries. / No, I can't. I can't deep fry French fries.

4. **Q:** Can you grill hamburgers?
   A: Yes, I can. I can grill hamburgers. / No, I can't. I can't grill hamburgers.
5. **Q:** Can you bake muffins?
   A: Yes, I can. I can bake muffins. / No, I can't. I can't bake muffins.
6. **Q:** Can you make coffee?
   A: Yes, I can. I can make coffee. / No, I can't. I can't make coffee.
7. **Q:** Can you fry an egg?
   A: Yes, I can. I can fry an egg. / No, I can't. I can't fry an egg.
8. **Q:** Can you steam a bun?
   A: Yes, I can. I can steam a bun. / No, I can't. I can't steam a bun.

2 1. do, have to   2. Does, have to
3. Do, have to   4. Do, have to
5. Does, have to   6. do, have to

3 1. May I   2. Can I / May I   3. Could you
4. Shall I   5. Would you   6. I'll
7. How about   8. Would you

4 1. Would you like something to drink?
2. Would you like an alcoholic beverage?
3. Would you like some juice?
4. Would you like a cup of coffee or tea?
5. Would you like a bag of nuts?

5 1. I can't walk to work.
2. Susie couldn't dance all night.
3. I don't have to go to Joe's house tonight.
4. I don't have to go to see the doctor tomorrow.
5. I may not go on a vacation in August.
6. I might not go see the Picasso exhibit at the museum.
7. My friend can't sit in the full lotus position.
8. I can't finish all my homework this weekend.
9. I don't have to stop eating beans.
10. John doesn't have to see Joseph.
11. The turtle may not win the race against the rabbit.
12. My friend Jon shouldn't get a different job.

6 1. Can you fry an egg?
2. Could Paul swim out to the island?
3. Must John go to Japan? / Does John have to go to Japan?
4. Does Abby have to go to the studio?
5. Can George play the guitar?
6. Must David finish his homework before he goes outside to play?
7. Do they have to cross the road?
8. Do I have to give away my concert tickets?
9. Does Joan have to stay at home tomorrow night?

7 1. A   2. A   3. C   4. A   5. A   6. A   7. A
8. C   9. B   10. B

8 1. A   2. D   3. H   4. C   5. F   6. B   7. G   8. E

9 1. must be   2. must visit
3. must be, must eat   4. must pay
5. mustn't play

10 1. may have, should not eat
2. may listen, should not download
3. may have, should not put
4. may drive, may not find
5. may call, may not answer
6. may watch, must not try

11 1. should give   2. shouldn't feed
3. should adopt   4. shouldn't give
5. should spend   6. should take

Unit 71 p. 61

1 1. James isn't playing with his new iPhone.
2. Vincent doesn't own a shoe factory.
3. They didn't go to a concert last night.
4. I don't enjoy reading.
5. I can't ride a unicycle.
6. Summer vacation won't begin soon.
7. I didn't have a nightmare last night.
8. I'm not from Vietnam.

2 1. Sue watched the football game on TV last night.
2. Rick can speak Japanese.
3. Phil and Jill were at the office yesterday.
4. I could enter the house this morning.
5. Joseph likes spaghetti.
6. They are drinking apple juice.
7. She is going shopping tomorrow.
8. I will tell Sandy.

Unit 72 p. 63

1 1. Is Jerry good at photography?
2. Doesn't Jane believe what he said?
3. Did he ever show up at the party?
4. Does Johnny get up early every day?
5. Will I remember you?
6. Did Julie ask me to give her a ride yesterday?
7. Was she surprised when he called?
8. Is he going to buy a gift tomorrow?

2 1. What are you watching on the Internet?
2. What are you interested in?
3. Who is that man?
4. Who is your favorite musician?
5. What is he looking at?
6. Who is writing an email?

Unit 73   p. 65

1 1. Who ate my slice of pizza?
What did Johnny eat?
2. Who consulted Lauren first?
Who did the boss consult first?
3. Who helped cook the fish?
What did Tom help cook?
4. Who broke the vase?
What did my dog break?
5. Who is making food for the baby?
Who is Mom making food for?
6. Who is standing next to Allen?
Who is Denise standing next to?

Unit 74   p. 67

1 **which:** this one, the blue shirt, the large one, the taller man
where: Italy, the office, the mall, the garage
when: tomorrow, last December, in 2022, next month
whose: Amber's, my brother's, Ms. Smith's, the cat's
2 1. When   2. Where   3. Which   4. Whose
5. Where   6. When   7. Whose   8. When
9. Which   10. When

Unit 75   p. 69

1 1. How old   2. How tall   3. How much
4. How many   5. How   6. How often
7. How long   8. How old   9. How
10. How tall   11. How much   12. How often
13. How long   14. How

Unit 76   p. 71

1 1. can't I   2. aren't you   3. do I   4. can't I
5. do you   6. have I   7. didn't you
8. did you   9. did you   10. haven't you
11. do you   12. do you
2 1. aren't you   2. is he   3. can you
4. won't she   5. didn't I   6. does she
7. isn't it   8. aren't I   9. isn't it   10. did he

Unit 77   p. 73

1 1. ✓   2. -   3. ✓   4. -   5. ✓   6. ✓   7. -
8. ✓   9. -   10. ✓
2 1. Paul, close that door.
2. Don't go out at midnight.
3. Don't throw garbage into the toilet.
4. Go buy some eggs now.
5. Don't be mad at me.
6. Take a No. 305 bus to the city hall.
7. Be careful not to wake up the baby.
8. Don't worry about so many things.

9. Relax.
10. Do your homework right now.

Unit 78 Review Test   p. 74

1 1. N   2. A   3. N   4. Q   5. N   6. Q   7. A
8. Q   9. Q   10. A
2 1. When   2. Where   3. Who   4. How
5. Who   6. Where   7. When   8. How
9. Why   10. Why   11. Which   12. What
13. Which   14. What   15. Whose   16. Whose
3 1. Who is visiting Charles?
2. Who is Eve visiting?
3. Who wants to meet Cathy?
4. Who does Cathy want to meet?
5. What took Mary such a long time?
6. What did he take with him?
7. Who is Keith dating?
8. What crashed?
9. Who answered the phone?
10. Who wants to marry Jenny?
11. What does Dennis want to buy?
12. Who wants to buy a new cell phone?
13. Who wants to eat peanuts?
14. What does Sylvia want to eat?
4 1. isn't it?   2. is it?   3. aren't they?
4. are we?   5. didn't you?   6. did you?
7. wasn't it   8. was it?   9. didn't you?
5 1. Who is Chris calling?
2. What does Irene want to do?
3. Who wants to stay for dinner?
4. Who finished the last piece of cake?
5. Who invented the automobile?
6. Whose dirty dishes are these on the table?
7. Which side of the road do you drive on?
8. Rupert likes history, doesn't he?
9. They drive a minivan, don't they?
6 **Bob:** How can I get to the station?
Eve: **Go** straight down this road. **Walk** for fifteen minutes and you will see a park.
Bob: So the station is near the park?
Eve: Yes. **Turn** right at the park and **walk** for another five minutes. **Cross** the main road. The station will be at your left. You won't miss it.
Bob: That's very helpful of you.
Eve: **Be** sure not to take any small alleys on the way.
Bob: I won't. Thank you very much.
Eve: You're welcome.
7 1. Eddie isn't a naughty boy.
Is Eddie a naughty boy?
2. Jack doesn't walk to work every morning.
Does Jack walk to work every morning?

7

3. Sammi didn't visit Uncle Lu last Saturday.
   Did Sammi visit Uncle Lu last Saturday?
4. She won't be able to finish the project next week.
   Will she be able to finish the project next week?
5. My boss isn't going to Beijing tomorrow.
   Is my boss going to Beijing tomorrow?
6. Joe hasn't seen the show yet.
   Has Joe already seen the show?

Unit 79 — p. 79

1 1. come along   2. work out   3. hang out
   4. taken off   5. stay up   6. moving in
   7. Come in
2 1. true   2. out   3. up   4. up   5. in   6. down
   7. off   8. down   9. up   10. up   11. on   12. up

Unit 80 — p. 81

1 1. set off
   → Dick and Byron set the fire crackers off.
   → Dick and Byron set them off.
   2. take off
   → Don't take the price tag off in case we have to return the sweater.
   → Don't take it off in case we have to return the sweater.
   3. turn down
   → Don't turn the offer down right away.
   → Don't turn it down right away.
   4. throw away
   → We don't throw bottles away if they can be recycled.
   → We don't throw them away if they can be recycled.
   5. fill out
   → You need to fill the form out and attach two photos.
   → You need to fill it out and attach two photos.
   6. try on
   → Would you like to try these shoes on?
   → Would you like to try them on?
   7. turn off
   → Could you turn the radio off? I don't want to listen to it.
   → Could you turn it off? I don't want to listen to it.
   8. call off
   → I'll have to call the meeting off.
   → I'll have to call it off.
   9. brought up
   → Lucy brought her son up by herself.
   → Lucy brought him up by herself.

Unit 81 — p. 83

1 1. look after   2. Watch out for   3. catch up with
   4. put up with   5. come across
   6. fed up with   7. run down   8. get over
2 1. on, off   2. in/into   3. into   4. to   5. out of
   6. of   7. for   8. on   9. to   10. in   11. for

Unit 82 Review Test — p. 84

1 1. wake, up   2. hang out   3. take off, get on
   4. hand in   5. threw away   6. move in
   7. Get in   8. Keep away from   9. fill out
   10. getting along with   11. keep up with
   12. pick up   13. grew up   14. brought up
   15. working out   16. call off   17. hung up
   18. try on
2 1. looking for   2. Look up   3. look after
   4. Look out   5. turn down   6. turn on
   7. turn down   8. turn off   9. take out
   10. Take off   11. take off   12. take after
   13. put on   14. put out   15. put off
   16. put away   17. go on   18. went off
   19. went out

Unit 83 — p. 87

1 1. old pants   2. new pants   3. soft chair
   4. hard chair   5. big dog   6. small dog
   7. curved road   8. straight road
2 1. He lives in a small town.
   2. She has blue eyes.
   3. The lamb stew smells good.
   4. I have two lovely kids.
   5. My teddy bear is cute.

Unit 84 — p. 89

1 1. suddenly   2. really   3. early   4. quickly
   5. well   6. finally   7. fast   8. lazily
   9. entirely   10. gently   11. luckily
   12. cheaply   13. probably   14. specially
   15. cheerfully   16. deeply   17. merrily
   18. clean   19. simply   20. angrily
2 1. He answered clearly.
   2. He sings badly.
   3. He arrived at school late. / He arrived late for school.
   4. She paints well.
   5. She learns fast.
   6. He works noisily.
   7. She translates professionally.
   8. The earth trembled terribly.
   9. She reads fast.
   10. She shops frequently.

Unit 85   p. 91

1
1. My parents live over there.
2. They bought the house over 20 years ago.
3. My dad pays the mortgage to the bank on the first day of each month.
4. He went downstairs to check the mailbox.
5. No packages were delivered to Wendy's house this morning.
6. Jack and Jimmy are going to meet at the café this afternoon.

2
1. I left the bag in the cloakroom at 4:30 yesterday.
2. I last saw him at Teresa's birthday party on January 22nd.
3. I bought that book at the bookstore around the corner last week.
4. I go swimming at the health club on Sundays.
5. I learned to dive at the Pacific Diving Club three years ago.
6. I ate lunch at Susie's Pizza House at 12:30 yesterday.

Unit 86   p. 93

1
1. He never misses the mortgage payment.
2. He is always the first customer in the morning.
3. He walks to work every day.
4. The water overflowed quickly. / The water quickly overflowed.
5. The volcano exploded suddenly. / The volcano suddenly exploded.
6. There have been many burglaries lately.
7. That changed their minds entirely.

2（答案略）

Unit 87   p. 95

1
1. bigger, biggest   2. taller, tallest
3. closer, closest   4. faster, fastest
5. sadder, saddest   6. cuter, cutest
7. spicier, spiciest   8. thinner, thinnest
9. better, best   10. more, most
11. larger, largest   12. later, latest
13. busier, busiest   14. simpler, simplest
15. tinier, tiniest   16. worse, worst
17. more useful, most useful   18. less, least
19. quieter, quietest   20. higher, highest

2（答句之答案略）
1. the cutest   2. the most hardworking
3. the funniest   4. the most boring
5. the most friendly   6. the tallest
7. the smartest   8. the most creative

Unit 88   p. 97

1
1. Ken is shorter than Jim.
2. Ken is more professional than Jim.
3. Ken is fatter than Jim.
4. Jim is taller than Ken.
5. Jim is more casual than Ken.
6. Ken is more business-like than Jim.
7. Ken is more intense than Jim.
8. Jim is more lighthearted than Ken.

2
1. ✗ Mt. Everest is the highest mountain in the world.
2. ✗ The Japan Trench is deeper than the Java Trench, but the Mariana Trench is the deepest.
3. ✗ Africa is not as large as Asia.
4. ✗ Blue whales are the largest animal in the world.
5. ✓
6. ✗ China is not as democratic as the United States.
7. ✗ The Burj Dubai is taller than Taipei 101.
8. ✓

Unit 89   p. 99

1
1. too noisy   2. too many   3. too dark
4. too busy   5. too talkative

2
1. It was too noisy for Charlie to talk on the phone.
2. There were too many phone calls for Amy to take a coffee break.
3. It was too dark for Andrew to see the keyboard very well.
4. Jessica was too busy to help her colleagues with their work.
5. Tony's colleagues were too talkative for him to concentrate on his work.

Unit 90 Review Test   p. 100

1
1. He is/looks strong.   2. He is/looks weak.
3. It is/looks tall.   4. She is/looks short.
5. He is/looks fat.   6. She is/looks healthy.
7. She is/looks happy.
8. She is/looks thoughtful.

2
1. clear   2. dearly   3. fair   4. just   5. wide
6. quickly   7. wrongly   8. slowly
9. carefully

3
1. He is a handsome guy.
2. That guy is handsome.
3. Ned takes the subway to his office.
4. Penny is always ready to take a break.
5. Dennis is a terrible driver.
6. Dennis drives terribly.
7. I'm too excited to wait.

8. This bag isn't big enough for these gifts.

9. Do you work here in this building?

10. Does Larry fight with his brother every day?

11. Did we meet at the Italian restaurant last Monday night?

12. Does Mr. Harrison always eat lunch at the same time?

13. Is Greg usually late for his tennis date?

14. Does Frederica go to the spa every week?

15. Are you sometimes too tired to get up in the morning?

4 1. every day   2. twice a week   3. often
4. sometimes   5. never

5 1. every Sunday   2. six times a month
3. always   4. every week   5. every weekend

6 1. ✗ I see two tall guys.
2. ✓
3. ✗ Tony is taller than David.
4. ✗ Who is the tallest guy in the room?
5. ✓
6. ✗ James is better at math than Robert.
7. ✗ Irving is a happy guy.
8. ✗ Janice speaks English very well.

7 1. quietly   2. joyfully   3. eagerly   4. slowly

8 1. Mt. Fuji isn't as tall as Mt. Everest.
2. Brazil isn't as big as Russia.
3. Madagascar isn't as big as Greenland.
4. Jakarta isn't as prosperous as Seoul.
5. Manila isn't as densely populated as Tokyo.
6. France isn't as small as Switzerland.
7. Iceland isn't as far south as Spain.
8. Italy isn't as far north as Germany.
9. Canada isn't as hot as Mexico.
10. Egypt isn't as cold as Sweden.

9 1. sweeter than   2. warmer than
3. hotter than   4. the coldest   5. the biggest
6. the tallest   7. as terrible as   8. as fast as
9. as high as

10 1. too hard / hard enough
2. too late
3. too salty / salty enough
4. too spicy / spicy enough
5. too blunt / blunt enough
6. too loud / loud enough
7. too expensive
8. too slow

Unit 91 p. 107

1 1. on   2. in   3. at   4. in   5. in   6. on
7. on   8. on   9. on

Unit 92 p. 109

1 1. in   2. at   3. in   4. in
2 1. in   2. on   3. on   4. at   5. in   6. in

Unit 93 p. 111

1 1. behind   2. next to   3. in   4. on
5. against, near   6. next to   7. in front of
8. on   9. under   10. over   11. between
12. against

Unit 94 p. 113

1 1. out of   2. into   3. up   4. on   5. around
6. out of   7. along   8. across   9. through
10. past   11. down   12. off

Unit 95 p. 115

1 **in:** the morning, the evening
on: Friday afternoons, National Day, the weekend, Sundays, Monday, Christmas Day
at: Christmas, night, 6 o'clock
2 1. at   2. on   3. in   4. at   5. on   6. on
7. at   8. on   9. on   10. on

Unit 96 p. 117

1 **in:** winter, October, 1998, the fall
on: May 5, June 27
✗: this weekend, tomorrow afternoon, next summer, yesterday morning, last month
2 1. in   2. on   3. in   4. on   5. in   6. ✗   7. ✗
8. on   9. in   10. in

Unit 97 p. 119

1 （答案略）
2 1. since   2. since   3. for   4. for   5. since
6. since   7. since   8. for   9. for   10. since
11. for   12. since
3 （答案略）

Unit 98 Review Test p. 120

1 1. behind   2. from   3. under   4. down
5. off   6. out of
2 1. in   2. on   3. on   4. on   5. into   6. out of
7. into   8. on   9. between   10. behind
11. over   12. in   13. along   14. past   15. in
16. against   17. near   18. under   19. to
20. down
3 1. on   2. on   3. at   4. at   5. at   6. to   7. in
8. in   9. at   10. on   11. in
4 1. on   2. at   3. on   4. in   5. at   6. on
7. on   8. at, on   9. in, on   10. in   11. in

5 1. under, on   2. in   3. in front of   4. behind
   5. near   6. opposite   7. next to   8. between
6 1. for   2. for   3. since   4. ago   5. for
   6. for   7. ago   8. for   9. since
7 1. Dana left an hour ago.
   2. Nancy walked out of the office thirty-five minutes ago.
   3. Victor called three hours ago.
   4. Julie came four days ago.
   5. It happened a month ago.
   6. We saw her a year ago.
8 1. ago   2. left   3. for   4. for   5. since
   6. since

Unit 99   p. 127

1 1. I like soda and potato chips.
   2. Do you want to leave at night or in the morning?
   3. I can't cook, but I can barbecue.
   4. I have been to Switzerland and New Zealand.
   5. She isn't a ballet dancer, but she is a great hip hop dancer.
   6. Tom says he is rich, but he always borrows money from me.
   7. Will you come this week or next week?
   8. Shall we sit in the front or in the back?
   9. I read comic books and novels.
   10. Do you like to eat German food or French food?

Unit 100   p. 129

1 1. If he lifts weights, he will build up his muscles.
   2. If she skips dessert, she will stay slim.
   3. If she often goes jogging, she will increase her stamina.
   4. If she reads widely, she'll learn lots of things.
   5. If he practices writing, he'll improve his communication skills.
   6. If he practices public speaking, he'll become self-confident.
2 1. When she finishes stretching, she'll start jogging.
   2. When she gets tired, she'll rest on a bench.
   3. When she gets home, she'll eat breakfast.

Unit 101 Review Test   p. 130

1 1. because my car broke down
   2. because my boss needed me to work late in the office
   3. so I could finish my report
   4. because I had to bake cookies

   5. because my dog was sick
   6. so I could see my favorite TV show
   7. because I had to take a sick friend to the hospital
   8. because I had to help my mom clean the house
2 1. and   2. but   3. or   4. and   5. but   6. or
   7. and   8. but   9. or   10. or
3 1. when   2. if   3. when   4. if   5. when
   6. if   7. When   8. If   9. when   10. If
4 1. When, will wear   2. If, will ask   3. when, ask
   4. If, will take   5. if, tell   6. When, will give
5 1. after, before   2. before   3. after
   4. before   5. after

Unit 102   p. 133

1 1. nine   2. thirteen   3. seventy-eight
   4. one hundred and forty-one
   5. three hundred and eighty-five
   6. seven thousand, and sixty-four
   7. nine thousand, eight hundred and fifty-six
   8. ten thousand, two hundred and thirty-one
   9. one million, thirty-two thousand, five hundred and forty
   10. six million, eight hundred and thirty-seven thousand, six hundred and fifty
   11. forty million
   12. twelve million, four hundred and fifty-two thousand, six hundred and eighty-nine
2 1. nine one one
   2. eight seven eight six, five two three nine
   3. three one eight, dash, nine two six, dash, five two seven three
   4. zero zero three, dash, one, dash, two five zero, dash, seven six four, dash, five three two zero
   5. zero two, dash, three two seven six, dash, nine three seven zero
   6. zero nine three two, dash, five four zero, dash, six nine six
   7. two three six four, dash, five eight three nine, extension twelve

Unit 103   p. 135

1 1. the first   2. the third   3. the fourth
   4. the sixteenth   5. the twenty-ninth
   6. the thirty-second   7. the thirty-fifth
   8. the thirty-seventh   9. the forty-second
   10. the forty-fourth

Unit 104   p. 137

1 1. Mr. Simpson is meeting Ms. Miller on Monday.

2. Mr. Simpson is visiting his grandma on Tuesday.
3. Mr. Simpson is going shopping on Wednesday.
4. Mr. Simpson is having dinner with Tom on Thursday.
5. Mr. Simpson is picking up Peter at the airport on Friday.
6. Mr. Simpson is playing basketball on Saturday.
7. Mr. Simpson is going to the movies on Sunday.
2 1. the twentieth of May, nineteen ninety-nine
2. the nineteenth of June, nineteen ninety-six
3. the first of March, two thousand eighteen
4. the eleventh of October, fifteen oh two
5. the twenty-sixth of February, two thousand ten
6. the thirty-first of December, eighteen seventy-six

Unit 105   p. 139

1 1. D   2. E   3. A   4. F   5. C   6. B
2 1. It's a quarter past nine. It's nine fifteen.
2. It's three o'clock. / It's 3 p.m. / It's 3 a.m.
3. It's half past three. It's three thirty.
4. It's a quarter to three.
It's fifteen minutes to three.
It's two forty-five.
5. It's seven oh two.
It's two minutes past seven.
6. It's five thirty-nine.
It's twenty-one minutes to six.
7. It's ten nineteen.
It's nineteen minutes past ten.

Unit 106 Review Test   p. 140

1 1. January, February   2. Sunday   3. March
4. August   5. Sunday   6. Thursday
7. Friday   8. July, August, September
9. Thursday, November   10. May, June
2 1. the twenty-fifth of December
2. the thirty-first of December
3. the first of January
4. the fourteenth of February
5. the fifth of May
6. the seventh of July
7. the fifteenth of August
8. the thirty-first of October
9. the twenty-nine of February
3 1. eight nine three zero seven six three five
2. zero two, dash, three four seven eight nine seven one one

3. eight eight six, dash, two, dash, one one five, dash, six seven three zero
4. four five six one eight nine three two, extension one one two
5. zero nine six five three two one five seven eight
6. the twenty-eighth of March / March (the) twenty-eighth
7. the fourth of July / July (the) fourth
8. the first of January / January (the) first
9. the eighteenth of September / September (the) eighteenth
10. fourteen fifty-nine
11. nineteen thirty-eight
12. two thousand nine
13. two thousand twenty

Progress Test

Part 6   p. 142

1 1. use   2. to use   3. to use / using   4. finish
5. call   6. to see   7. stuff / to stuff   8. to start
9. starting   10. to send   11. to learn
12. to learn   13. playing   14. to turn
15. holding
2 1. for   2. for   3. to   4. to

Part 7   p. 142

1 1. shopping   2. started   3. to fix   4. do
5. deliver   6. mailed   7. to walk
2 1. a swim   2. a trip   3. taking   4. of
5. from   6. have   7. do, do   8. place

Part 8   p. 143

1 1. can   2. can   3. can   4. can't   5. Can you
2 1. ✓   2. ✓
3. ✗ If I could I would, but I can't so I won't.
4. ✗ He could climb up trees when he was young, but he couldn't get down.
5. ✓
3 1. must tell   2. must pay   3. mustn't eat
4. must call
4 1. shouldn't make   2. should leave
3. should see   4. should ask
5 1. must / have to   2. must   3. has to
4. has to   5. have to   6. must
6 1. Can you check the balance in my account?
2. Could I please transfer $20,000?
3. Could you go over the charges for an electronic fund transfer?
4. May I use your pen to fill out this form?
5. May I have some extra copies of this EFT form?

6. Would you like me to give the baby a bath?
7. Would you like to take a break while I watch the baby?
8. I'll change the baby's diaper for you.
9. Should I warm up some milk for your baby?
10. Should I put the baby down for a nap?
7 1. Let's   2. Why don't we   3. shall
4. How about   5. shall   6. How about
7. Why don't we

Part 9 p. 145

1 1. Who   2. What   3. Which   4. Whose
5. Where   6. When   7. Why   8. How
9. How old   10. How often
2 1. What are you doing?
2. What is the movie about?
3. What happened to the daughter?
4. What happens at the end of the movie?
3 1. aren't you   2. isn't it   3. can he   4. am I
5. don't you   6. didn't he
4 1. Call   2. Move   3. come, sit   4. Don't take
5. Don't forget   6. pass

Part 10 p. 146

1 1. B   2. C   3. A   4. A   5. B   6. B   7. A   8. A
2 1. to   2. from   3. to   4. for   5. with   6. for

Part 11 p. 147

1 1. too sweet   2. loud enough   3. too bitter
4. very
2 1. ✓   2. ✗ It's a fast computer.   3. ✓
4. ✗ The machine is light.
3 1. I leave at 10:00.
2. Pick me up at my house at 7:00.
3. Greg always dresses up to go dancing.
4. Teddy is never the first to arrive.
5. The kids were playing at the park yesterday.
6. She ran to the car quickly five minutes ago. / She quickly ran to the car five minutes ago.
4 1. nicer, nicest   2. smaller, smallest
3. sadder, saddest   4. busier, busiest
5. prettier, prettiest   6. better, best
7. worse, worst   8. more, most
9. more important, most important
10. more popular, most popular
11. more successful, most successful
12. more boring, most boring
5 1. smooth   2. smoothly   3. awful
4. earnest   5. incredibly   6. artificially

6 1. bad   2. worse   3. worst   4. tight
5. tighter   6. tightest   7. important
8. more important   9. most important

Part 12 p. 149

1 1. on, in   2. on   3. at, at   4. at, in
5. in, at/in   6. at, in
2 1. at, at   2. in, at   3. on   4. on, in   5. ✗, ✗
3 1. near, in front of   2. next to, opposite
3. into, out of   4. to, off   5. up, down
6. through, across   7. over, under
8. past, around, between   9. to, from
4 1. ✗ They left for lunch an hour ago.   2. ✓
3. ✓   4. ✗ I have been shopping for an hour.
5. ✓   6. ✓

Part 13 p. 150

1 1. when   2. if/when   3. if   4. When
5. When   6. If
2 1. and   2. and   3. but   4. or   5. because
6. so
3 1. because   2. so   3. because   4. because
5. so   6. because   7. so   8. because
9. so   10. because

Part 14 p. 151

1 1. thirty-four
2. one hundred and forty-three
3. one thousand, eight hundred, and ninety-five
4. eight thousand
5. zero three, three four five nine eight four three one
6. ninth and tenth
7. the twentieth of April / April (the) twentieth
8. eight o'clock
9. eight thirty / half past eight / thirty minutes past eight
10. eight oh eight / eight minutes past eight
11. eight forty-five / fifteen to nine / a quarter to nine
2 1. Monday, Tuesday   2. January, February
3. weekend   4. autumn/fall   5. in, at

Part 12   Prepositions 介系詞

Part 13   Conjunctions 連接詞

Part 14   Numbers, Time, and Dates 數字、時間和日期

Basic 1

Part 6 Infinitives and -ing Forms
不定詞和動詞的 -ing 形式

Unit 50

Infinitives (1)
不定詞（1）

1 動詞有三種型態：不加 to 的不定詞、加 to 的不定詞、動名詞。

I can play the guitar. 我會彈吉他。

I want to play the guitar. 我想要彈吉他。

I enjoy playing the guitar.
我喜歡彈吉他。

不加 to 的不定詞 （動詞原形）	加 to 的不定詞	V-ing
be	to be	being
play	to play	playing
work	to work	working

2 「不加 to 的不定詞」在形式上就是**動詞原形**，像是助動詞 do/does/did 和情態助動詞 can/may/will 等，後面都會接「不加 to 的不定詞（動詞原形）」。

My son can ride a bicycle.
我兒子會騎腳踏車。

We could eat crawfish for dinner.
我們晚餐可以吃小龍蝦。

She may start a new dance class.
她可能會開一個新的舞蹈班。

Did you go to the concert yesterday?
你昨天有去聽音樂會嗎？

Shall we call Grandmother after dinner?
晚飯後我們要不要打電話給奶奶？

3 「加 to 的不定詞」在形式上就是「to + 動詞原形」，許多動詞像是 decide、hope、learn、want、would like 等等，後面都會接「加 to 的不定詞」。

I can't **afford** to waste any time.
我沒有時間可以浪費。

I **decided** to start a new company.
我決定開一間新公司。

I **expect** to hit the big time any day now.
我隨時期待能飛黃騰達。

I **have** to learn many things about being in business.
關於生意方面的事，我有很多要學的。

I **learned** to chew gum and drink a soda at the same time.
我在還只能喝汽水的年紀就會嚼口香糖了。

I **promise** to remember you when I'm rich and famous.
我答應你，在我功成名就之後，還是會記得你。

I **hope** to retire at the age of 50.
我希望能在 50 歲的時候退休。

- David [1] _____ a new tablet.
  大衛想買一個新的平板電腦。
- Joanne [2] _____ 300 English words every week.
  瓊安希望每週能學 300 個英文單字。

Practice

1

將括弧內的動詞以正確的形式填空。

1. I may _____ (watch) a football game this weekend.
2. I learned _____ (play) baseball last summer.
3. I can't _____ (fly) a kite.
4. He promised _____ (give) me a call when he arrives in London.
5. Mike hates _____ (go) to meetings.
6. Kate would like _____ (win) the race in the sports event on Sunday.
7. Did you _____ (hear) what she said?
8. I can _____ (play) baseball.
9. I will _____ (go) on an outing tomorrow.
10. I promise _____ (be) a good guy.
11. I want _____ (meet) your parents.

2

依據圖示，自右表選出適當的動詞片語，以正確的形式填空。

pay the bill	quit drinking and smoking
look very happy	wear clothes
buy some red peppers	make good coffee
work 10 hours a day	

1

She'd like _____
_____.

2

Help Joe _____
_____.

3

Ms. Jones can _____
_____.

4

Little Kuku does not _____.

Maybe he doesn't want _____.

5

Jennifer has _____
_____.

6

He would like _____
_____.

Part 6 Infinitives and -ing Forms
不定詞和動詞的 -ing 形式

Unit 51

Infinitives (2)
不定詞（2）

1 有些片語後面一定接「不加 to 的不定詞（動詞原形）」，例如：let's 和 Why don't we。

Let's go to the beach. 我們去海邊吧。

Why don't we walk on the barrier island?
我們何不到沙洲島上走走？

2 有些動詞通常先接受詞，再接「加 to 的不定詞」。

① ask 要求　　⑤ tell 吩咐
② expect 要求　⑥ want 要
③ invite 邀請　⑦ allow 允許
④ teach 教　　⑧ would like 想要

I asked Joan to call my wife.
我請瓊打電話給我太太。

The dean expects you to publish two papers. 院長希望你能夠發表兩篇論文。

Howard invited us to join the tour group.
霍華邀請我們參加旅行團。

Please teach me to dribble the ball.
請教教我如何運球。

The doctor told the patient to drink lots of water. 醫生要這名病人多喝水。

Mom doesn't allow me to go out because I'm sick.
我生病了，媽媽不讓我出去玩。

3 有些動詞，後面可接「不加 to 的不定詞」，也可以接「加 to 的不定詞」，意思都一樣，例如：help。

We'll help eat the leftovers.
= We'll help to eat the leftovers.
我們會幫忙把剩菜吃完。

help 後面如果有受詞，則會先接受詞，再接兩種不定詞。

Can you help me cook dinner?
= Can you help me to cook dinner?
你可以幫忙我煮晚餐嗎？

4 有些形容詞後需接「加 to 的不定詞」。

① easy 容易的　　⑤ expensive 昂貴的
② difficult 困難的　⑥ stupid 愚蠢的
③ important 重要的　⑦ too 太……
④ possible 可能的　⑧ enough 足夠的

It's difficult to play chess.
玩西洋棋很難。

It is important to eat fruit every day.
每天吃水果很重要。

It isn't possible to drive to Hawaii from California. 從加州開車到夏威夷是不可能的。

I had too much to eat. 我已經吃不下了。

I had enough to drink. 我已經喝夠了。

5 不定代名詞 something、anything 或 nowhere 等，後面也可以接「加 to 的不定詞」。

I have something to tell him.
我有些事要跟他說。

She doesn't have anything to say.
她沒有任何話要說。

Practice

1

請填入正確的動詞形態，有些動詞有兩種正確的型態。

1. I want you _____ (finish) cleaning the house in thirty minutes.
2. Let's _____ (go) out to dinner.
3. Why don't we _____ (sit) on the sofa?
4. Please teach me _____ (fly) your airplane.
5. Let's invite your sister _____ (join) the party.
6. I want you _____ (call) her right now.
7. Would you like me _____ (call) her for you?
8. Can I help you _____ (make) some more phone calls?
9. It's easy _____ (have) a party.
10. This house is too small _____ (throw) a party.
11. There's nowhere _____ (sit) .

2

依據圖示，自右表選出適當的詞彙，以正確的動詞型態填空。

bake cookies	read a story to you
finish the paper today	study for the exam
get the sausage on the plate	take a look at your answers
climb a tree	eat on a train

1. Is it possible

_____ ?

2. Let me

_____ .

3. It's stupid

_____ .

4. Am I allowed

_____ ?

5. It's fun

_____ .

6. I'm too tired

_____ .

7. Do you want me

_____ ?

8. Professor Butler expects us _____ .

Part 6 Infinitives and -ing Forms
不定詞和動詞的 -ing 形式

Unit 52

-ing Forms
動詞的 -ing 形式

1 V-ing 形式經常被稱為**動名詞**,同時具有**動詞**和**名詞**的性質。有些動詞和片語動詞後面再接的動詞,必須是 V-ing。

① **enjoy** 享受　④ **imagine** 想像
② **finish** 完成　⑤ **give up** 放棄
③ **mind** 介意　⑥ **feel like** 想要

I <u>enjoy</u> <u>listening</u> to classical music.
我喜歡聽古典音樂。

He <u>finished</u> <u>writing</u> his first novel.
他完成了他的第一本小說。

I don't <u>mind</u> <u>sitting</u> in the dark.
我不介意坐在黑暗中。

Can you <u>imagine</u> <u>living</u> on the moon?
你能想像住在月球上的生活嗎?

Maggie wants to <u>give up</u> <u>playing</u> the piano. 瑪姬想要放棄彈鋼琴。

Do you <u>feel like</u> <u>going</u> to a movie?
你想不想去看電影?

2 談論活動時,常用「go + V-ing」的形式。(詳見 Unit 55 說明)

He <u>went hiking</u> in Switzerland.
他去瑞士健行。

We're <u>going swimming</u> at Silver Lake.
我們要到銀湖去游泳。

I <u>go surfing</u> in Indonesia every year.
我每年都到印尼去衝浪。

3 有些**介系詞**後面的動詞要用 V-ing 的型態。

① at　② in　③ for　④ about　⑤ before

What <u>about</u> <u>calling</u> me when you finish?
等你結束後,打個電話給我如何?

I'm not very good <u>at</u> <u>finding</u> my way around a new city.
我不太擅長在新城市裡找到路。

Are you interested <u>in</u> <u>helping</u> me find out what happened?
你有興趣幫我查明發生什麼事了嗎?

This map is good <u>for</u> <u>finding</u> streets near the train station.
這個地圖可以幫你尋找火車站周邊的街道。

I will call <u>before</u> <u>leaving</u> in case you are free.
我會在出發前先打通電話,確認你有空。

4 有些**動詞**後面可以接「加 to 的不定詞」,也可以接 V-ing,意思都一樣。

① like 喜歡　④ start 開始
② love 愛　⑤ begin 開始
③ hate 恨

Tommy <u>loves</u> <u>listening</u> to the blues.
= Tommy <u>loves</u> <u>to listen</u> to the blues.
湯米喜歡聽藍調音樂。

Kevin <u>started</u> <u>learning</u> how to fly a drone.
= Kevin <u>started</u> <u>to learn</u> how to fly a drone.
凱文開始學習如何使用空拍機。

John <u>hates</u> <u>eating</u> vegetables.
= John <u>hates</u> <u>to eat</u> vegetables.
約翰不喜歡吃蔬菜。

Practice

1

依據圖示，自右表選出
適當的動詞，以「V-ing
的形式」填空。

play soccer	wait for his master
draw on canvas	sing a song
blow bubbles	bike
make clothes	walk in the rain

1 He is good at

_____

_____ .

2 She is interested in

_____

_____ .

3 She loves

_____

_____ .

4 He feels like

_____

_____ .

5 He enjoys

_____

_____ .

6 She went _____

_____ with

her friend yesterday.

7 Gordon never gives up

_____

_____ .

8 She doesn't mind

_____

_____ .

2

請填入正確的動詞形
態，有些動詞有兩種
正確的形態。

1. Can I help you _____ (call) your family?

2. It's possible _____ (avoid) spending a lot of money.

3. I feel like _____ (drink) a Coke now.

4. I hate _____ (get up) early in the morning.

5. I'm not good at _____ (swim) .

6. Do you mind _____ (share) the table with this lady?

7. How about _____ (go) to Hong Kong with me?

8. He can't imagine _____ (live) a life without her.

9. I went _____ (run) twice last week.

10. I love _____ (go) to the movies.

11. Get all the papers ready before _____ (meet)

    with Mr. Lee.

12. Have you finished _____ (eat) your breakfast?

Purpose: "to . . ." and "for . . ."
to 和 for 表示目的的用法

1 加 to 的不定詞可用來說明「**某人做某事的原因**」。

I am going to the market to buy some food. 我要去市場買些食物。

On winter mornings I eat oatmeal to stay warm.
冬天的早晨，我會吃燕麥粥來保持溫暖。

- Mindy went to the convenience store
1 _____ some drinks.
敏蒂去便利商店買了一些飲料。
- Josh ran to her office 2 _____
her the news.
喬許跑去她的辦公室，告訴她這個消息。

2 「for + 名詞」也可用來解釋「**某人做某事的原因**」。

He wants to buy a new suit for his interview.
他想要買套新西裝去參加面試。

She needs to get a second battery for her cell phone.
她需要買一顆手機的備用電池。

- Wendy is studying hard
3 _____ .
溫蒂為了考試正在用功讀書。
- My brothers are fighting with each other
4 _____ .
我的兄弟們正為了新玩具
打得不可開交。

3 「for + V-ing」則用來表示「**東西的用途**」。

A fax machine is for sending copies of documents over phone lines.
傳真機是透過電話線，傳送文件的複本。

FTP software is for transferring computer files over networks.
FTP 軟體可以透過電腦網路系統，傳輸電腦裡的檔案。

錯誤

for 不能接不定詞。
✗ I am running for to exercise.
我跑步是為了要運動。

表達**目的**時，用「加 to 的不定詞」或「for + 名詞」的**意義相同**。

- I run every day to get some exercise.
  = I run every day for exercise.
  我每天跑步是為了要運動。
- He went to the health club to swim.
  = He went to the health club for a swim.
他到健身房去游泳。

比較

- Running is a good method for exercising.
  跑步是運動的一種好方式。

Practice

1

自右欄選出適當的詞彙來搭配左欄的地點，並正確選用「加 to 的不定詞」或「for + 名詞」的句型填空。

a library

1. You go to *a library to borrow books*   .

fun

a history museum

2. You go to ....

look at paintings

the aquarium

3. You go to ....

see the animals

an art gallery

4. You go to ....

see artifacts

the amusement park

5. You go to ....

borrow books

a zoo

6. You go to ....

see the fish

2

自框內選出適當的動詞，用「for + V-ing」的形式說明右列交通工具的用途。

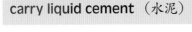

tow cars **and trucks**

put out **fires**

push soil **and rocks**

take the **sick or wounded to** the hospital

carry liquid cement （水泥）

1. A cement truck is a vehicle
....

2. A fire truck is a vehicle
....

3. A tow truck is a vehicle
....

4. An ambulance is a vehicle
....

5. A bulldozer is a vehicle
....

15

Unit **54** Review Test of Units 50–53
單元 50–53 總複習

1 將提示動詞以正確動詞型態填空。
→ Unit 50–52 重點複習

surf

1. I can _____ near my home in California.
2. I learned _____ during high school.
3. I love _____ and I go _____ every weekend.

ski

4. I might _____ this weekend.
5. I want _____ on Saturday afternoon.
6. We often go _____ on Mount Killington.

drive

7. Let's _____ for a while.
8. I'll help _____ if you get tired.
9. How about _____ into the city tomorrow?
10. It's easy _____ on the highway.

2 將下列句子以「加 to 的不定詞」或「for + 名詞」互相改寫。
→ Unit 53 重點複習

1. My parents went out to walk.
   → _My parents went out for a walk._

2. Mr. Lyle went to the front desk to pick up his package.
   → _____

3. I have to get everything ready to attend the meeting.
   → _____

4. I jog every day for my health.
   → _____

5. I walked into the McDonald's on Tenth Street for two cheeseburgers.
   → _____

3 選出正確的答案。

→ **Unit 50–53** 重點複習

.... 1. Do you enjoy .... in cold water?

Ⓐ swim   Ⓑ to swim   Ⓒ swimming

.... 2. I don't .... coffee at night.

Ⓐ drink   Ⓑ to drink   Ⓒ drinking

.... 3. Clive hopes .... promoted in six months.

Ⓐ get   Ⓑ to get   Ⓒ getting

.... 4. Why don't we .... the baseball game on channel 74?

Ⓐ watch   Ⓑ to watch   Ⓒ watching

.... 5. How about .... a trip to France?

Ⓐ take   Ⓑ to take   Ⓒ taking

.... 6. Can you help me .... the dishes?

Ⓐ did   Ⓑ to do   Ⓒ doing

.... 7. Do you mind .... for fifteen minutes?

Ⓐ wait   Ⓑ to wait   Ⓒ waiting

.... 8. My father taught me .... tennis when I was eight.

Ⓐ play   Ⓑ to play   Ⓒ playing

.... 9. He is depressed and wants to give up .... to college.

Ⓐ go   Ⓑ to go   Ⓒ going

.... 10. Jessie told me .... the secret.

Ⓐ keep   Ⓑ to keep   Ⓒ keeping

.... 11. It's difficult .... Russian.

Ⓐ learn   Ⓑ to learn   Ⓒ learning

.... 12. I have nothing .... at the moment.

Ⓐ say   Ⓑ to say   Ⓒ saying

.... 13. I would like you .... the car on Monday.

Ⓐ return   Ⓑ to return   Ⓒ returning

.... 14. Do you want me .... the window?

Ⓐ open   Ⓑ to open   Ⓒ opening

.... 15. Are you interested in .... horror movies?

Ⓐ watch   Ⓑ to watch   Ⓒ watching

4 將圖片中的詞彙與地點搭配，並正確選用「加 to 的不定詞」或「for + 名詞」的句型填空。
→ Unit 19–21 重點複習

the beach | play beach volleyball

1. They went to *the beach to play beach volleyball* .

the water | get the ball

2. The dog jumped into ....

the supermarket | some milk

3. They walked into ....

the opera house | a concert

4. They went to ....

the store | buy a gift

5. They went to ....

my friend's house | see her new doll house

6. I went to ....

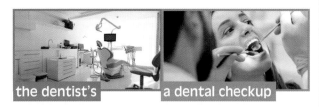

the dentist's | a dental checkup

7. She went to ....

the Starbucks | a cup of latté

8. She went to ....

the stadium | watch a baseball game

9. Andy went to ....

the market | buy some pumpkins

10. They went to ....

5 將錯誤的句子打✕，並寫出正確的句子。若句子無誤，則在方框內打✓。
→ Unit 50–53 重點複習

1. I might play basketball tonight.

   ☐ _____

2. I should to visit my sister.

   ☐ _____

3. Let's to go to see a movie.

   ☐ _____

4. I'll help make dinner.

   ☐ _____

5. I'll help to make dinner.

   ☐ _____

6. I want you call me next week.

   ☐ _____

7. Would you like that me to call you next week?

   ☐ _____

8. It's expensive to buy French wine.

   ☐ _____

9. When you finish to playing cards, call me.

   ☐ _____

10. I go to swimming every morning at 6:00.

    ☐ _____

11. Thank you for paying your rent on time.

    ☐ _____

12. Most people love to going on a vacation.

    ☐ _____

13. Ernie hates to eat liver and onions.

    ☐ _____

14. Kelly went to see the doctor for to have a checkup.

    ☐ _____

15. Kim went to the shop for some fresh sausages.

    ☐ _____

Unit **55**

Go
動詞 **Go** 的用法

- **go jogging** 去慢跑
- **go camping** 去露營
- **go mountain climbing** 去爬山
- **go hiking** 去健行
- **go dancing** 去跳舞
- **go swimming** 去游泳
- **go bowling** 去打保齡球

1 「**go + V-ing**」常用來表達「**從事某種活動**」。

My father used to go fishing with me on the weekends.
我父親過去經常週末和我去釣魚。

I'm going shopping **with Lucy this Saturday.**
這個星期六，我要跟露西去逛街。

2 **go for** 或 **go on** 加上某些名詞，也可以表達「**從事某種活動**」。

Would you like to go for a walk?
你想不想去散步？

Liz and John go for a swim every Sunday.
麗茲和約翰每週日都去游泳。

Who wants to **go on a picnic?**
　　　　　　↳ 強調 activity

= Who wants to **go for a picnic?**
誰想去野餐？　　↳ 強調 go 的「目的」

Sam went on a trip to New Zealand by himself for two weeks.
山姆獨自前往紐西蘭旅行了兩個禮拜。

go on +	a trip
	vacation / a vacation
	a picnic

go for +	a walk
	a ride
	a jog
	a swim

3 「**go + 形容詞**」可以表達「**變成某種狀態**」。

Everything went wrong! I don't know what to do.
什麼事都不對了！我不知道該怎麼辦。

The milk has gone sour. Don't drink it.
牛奶酸掉了，不要喝了。

go 的常用片語

go crazy 發瘋
I'm going crazy **with this project.**
這個案子真是令我抓狂。

go bad 腐壞
Tofu goes bad **easily if you don't put it in the refrigerator.**
如果你不把豆腐冷藏起來，它很快就會壞掉。

go by 時間過去
His memories of the old days faded as time went by.
隨著時光流逝，他的往日回憶也逐漸模糊。

go on 發生
What's going on? 發生什麼事了？

go Dutch 各自付帳
Let's go Dutch. 我們各付各的吧。

Practice

1

依據圖示，自下表選出正確的動詞，寫出「go + V-ing」的句型。

bowl

skate

ski

camp

sail

swim

go bowling

_____   _____

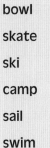

_____   _____

_____   _____

2

自下表選出適當的詞彙，以正確的形式填空。

go

go on

go for

go by

1. The leftover soup _____ bad. Don't eat it.
2. The weather is good. Let's _____ a ride.
3. Seven years _____ since his wife died, and he still strongly misses her.
4. There's too much homework. I'm _____ crazy.
5. How about _____ a jog tomorrow morning?
6. Philip and Linda _____ a vacation in Belgium last month.
7. Tony _____ boating with his brother yesterday.

Unit 56

Get and Take
動詞 Get 和 Take 的用法

1 「get + 受詞（人）+ 帶 to 的不定詞」可用來表達「**叫某人去做某件事**」。

Please get somebody to fix the toilet.
請找個人來修理馬桶。
I'll get him to give you a hand.
我會叫他去幫你。

2 「get + 受詞（物）+ 過去分詞」可用來表達「**使某物接受某個動作**」。

I'll get everything done as soon as possible.
我會盡快把所有的事情辦好。
Andrew, did you get the toilet fixed?
安德魯，你把馬桶修好了沒？

3 take 的基本意義是「**拿取**」，但它也有「**接受**」的意思。

Why don't you take Amanda's advice?
你何不接受雅曼達的建議呢？
I really want to take the job.
我是真的想接下這份工作。

4 take 經常用來表示「採取某種行動」。

Sally is taking a shower. 莎莉正在洗澡。
Would you like to take a look? 你要看一下嗎？
Take a seat, please. 請坐。

5 「take + 時間」用來表示「花費多少時間」。

It took me six years to get a medical degree. 我花了六年時間才拿到醫學學位。
It will take half an hour to get to the Central Station by bus.
搭公車去中央車站要半個小時。

get 的常用片語

get along 相處
I think I can get along with Zoe.
我想我應該可以跟柔伊相處得很好。

get over 克服
You will get over your homesickness.
你會克服你的鄉愁的。

get in 進入（汽車）
Get in the car now. 快上車。

get on 上車（火車、公車）
You can get on a No. 16 bus at the bus stop two blocks away. 你可以在兩個路口之後的公車站搭 16 路公車。

get off 下車（火車、公車）
Get off the train at the Central Station.
在中央車站就要下車。

get together 相聚
Ben and Tommy get together twice a month. 班和湯米每個月要聚會兩次。

take 的常用片語

take a picture 拍照
I took a picture of the scenery.
我把這景色拍下來了。

take care of 照顧
Sherry takes care of her grandparents.
雪莉一直照顧著她的祖父母。

take off 脫下衣物；起飛
Please take off your shoes before entering the house. 進屋子前請先脫鞋。
Our flight will take off in thirty minutes.
我們的班機將在 30 分鐘後起飛。

take part in 參與
Will you take part in the basketball game?
你會參加這場籃球賽嗎？

take place 發生
The accident took place in the middle of the night. 這場意外於夜半發生。

Practice

1

將括弧內的動詞以
正確的形式填空。

1. Marty, will you get Sam _____ (finish) his dinner?
2. I can't get my students _____ (listen) to me. I'm so upset.
3. I'll get a plumber _____ (fix) the faucet tomorrow.
4. I'll get the paper _____ (do) first thing in the morning.
5. I'll get my hair _____ (cut) tonight.
6. Are you going to get your car _____ (wash) tomorrow?

2

哪些名詞經常搭配
take 組成慣用片語？
請在方框內打 ✓。

take

☐ a shower   ☐ a walk   ☐ a nap   ☐ a jog

☐ a sleep   ☐ a look   ☐ a note   ☐ a smell

 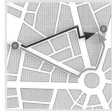  

☐ a picture   ☐ a shortcut   ☐ a chance   ☐ a seat

3

選出正確的答案。

1. **Get on / get in** the bus here, and **get out / get off** at the fifth stop.
2. It **got / took** me five hours to finish this report.
3. Let's work together and **get over / get away** this problem.
4. **Get off / Take off** your dirty clothes and throw them in the laundry basket.
5. We're eager to **get part in / take part in** this reconstruction project.
6. We haven't **gotten together / taken together** for three months because we're both busy.
7. She took care **about / of** her grandfather last winter.

Unit **57**

Do and Make
動詞 Do 和 Make 的用法

1 do 的基本意義是「做」，它的動詞三態是 do、did、done。

What are you doing? 你在做什麼？

I think Mandy did it on purpose.
我認為曼蒂是故意這樣做的。

Have you done your project for school?
你做完學校的案子了嗎？

do 的常用片語

do somebody a favor 幫某人的忙
Could you do me a favor, please?
你可以幫我一個忙嗎？

do one's best 盡力而為
Jessie did his best to find a home for the puppy.
傑西已經盡力幫那隻小狗找到家了。

do somebody good 對某人有益
Try to eat some fruit. It'll do you good.
吃點水果吧，那對身體好。

do exercise 做運動
My grandfather does exercise every morning. 我爺爺每天早上做運動。

do the dishes 洗碗
Andy, will you do the dishes tonight?
安迪，今晚你洗碗好嗎？

2 「make + somebody/something + 動詞原形」可以用來表示「使某人或某物做某個動作」。

I'll try to make him agree with this idea.
我會試著讓他同意這個主意。

Johnny's words made everyone in the room laugh.
強尼說的話讓屋子裡的每個人都笑了。

Is it possible to make it happen?
有可能讓這件事發生嗎？

3 「make + somebody + 形容詞／名詞」可以表示「使某人成為什麼樣的人物或狀態」。

Working hard will make you a successful person. 努力工作，你就會成功。

Brad tried so hard to make his wife happy.
布萊德已經很努力討好他太太。

make 的常用片語

make somebody something
幫某人做某樣東西
I'm making my sister a wedding dress.
我在幫我姊姊做一件結婚禮服。

make a mistake 犯錯
Don't blame yourself too much. Everyone makes mistakes. 別太自責了，人人都會犯錯。

make a decision 做決定
You have to make the decision right now.
你現在就必須做出決定。

be made from something
用什麼做的
（看不出材質的原形）

Paper is made from wood.
紙是用木材做的。

be made of something
用什麼做的
（看得出材質的原形）

This table is made of wood.
這張桌子是木製的。

Practice

1

自下表選出適當的詞彙，搭配 make 或 do 填空。

- a wish
- the decision
- a favor
- a mistake
- good
- a speech
- his best

1. Johnny, will you do me ＿＿＿＿＿ by helping me move this box away, please?

2. He made ＿＿＿＿＿ by sending the package to the wrong person.

3. Regular exercise will do you ＿＿＿＿＿.

4. Don't blame him. He has already done ＿＿＿＿＿.

5. After everyone sang Happy Birthday, she made ＿＿＿＿＿ and blew out the candles.

6. Jennifer is going to make ＿＿＿＿＿ at Toastmasters. She is practicing right now.

7. He has made ＿＿＿＿＿ to marry his girlfriend. It's impossible to change his mind.

2

選出正確的答案。

1. Amy, can you **do / make** the dishes right now?

2. I'm going to **do / make** you a sweater this winter.

3. Years of practice has **done / made** him a good snowboard player.

4. Does Kim **do / make** exercise every morning?

5. The rings are **made of / made from** silver.

6. Cheese is **made of / made from** milk.

7. Reading every day will do you **good / well**.

8. Those columns are **made of / made from** stone.

9. Can Professor Dune make the pig **fly / to fly**?

10. Hearing the bad news made her **sadness / sad**.

Unit 58

Have
動詞 Have 的用法

1 「have + somebody + 動詞原形」
表示「叫某人去做某件事」。

I'll have him call you back when he gets home. 等他回來，我就叫他回你電話。

The teacher had the students make up sentences using the verb "have".
老師讓學生們用 have 這個動詞造句。

2 「have + something + 過去分詞」
表示「讓某物接受某個動作」。

I'm going to have my hair cut.
我要去剪頭髮。

Joe had his sprained ankle taped up.
喬把他扭傷的腳踝包紮起來了。

We finally had the shower fixed.
我們終於把蓮蓬頭修好了。

比較

Jason, please have your son do his homework. ↳ 最委婉

= Jason, please make your son do his homework. ↳ 最強烈

= Jason, please get your son to do his homework.

傑森，叫你兒子去 做功課好嗎？
↳ 三個句子的意義差不多，
但用 have 的語氣最委婉，
用 make 最強烈。

have 常用片語

have a look 看一眼
Janet, come here and have a look at this.
珍奈特，過來看看這個。

have a walk 散步
My parents used to have a walk after dinner.
我父母以前晚餐後都會去散步。

have fun 玩得開心
Did you have fun in Bali?
你去峇里島玩得開心嗎？

have a good time 玩得開心
We had a good time last weekend.
我們上週末過得很開心。

have something to do with 與……有關
Does it have something to do with the professor?
這件事和教授有關嗎？

have nothing to do with 與……無關
It has nothing to do with me.
這件事與我無關。

have a baby 生小孩
Betty is going to have a baby next month.
貝蒂下個月就要生小孩了。

1 將下列句子以「have + somebody + 動詞原形」或
「have + something + 過去分詞」的形式改寫。

1. He shortened the pants.

   → ....

2. Yvonne got her son to mop the floor.

   → ....

3. She washed the car.

   → ....

4. She asked her husband to replace the light bulb.

   → ....

5. He folded the paper.

   → ....

6. She packed the box with the books and sent it to the professor.

   → ....

7. He made his students read thirty pages of the book a day.

   → ....

8. I'm going to wrap this gift.

   → ....

2

自右表選出正確的片語，
填空完成句子。

have a look	have a haircut
have a good time	have something to do with
have your baby	have nothing to do with

1. When are you going to ....?

2. Does it .... Jeff? I saw him leaving the building
   yesterday.

3. No, it .... Jeff. The police suspect someone else.

4. Can I .... at your new cell phone?

5. Did you .... on your last trip to New Zealand?

6. I'm thinking about .... tomorrow.

Review Test of Units 55–58
單元 55–58 總複習

1 選出正確的答案。

→ Unit 55–58 重點複習

........1. George and Lulu .... shopping yesterday.

   Ⓐ went   Ⓒ did   Ⓒ made

........2. It will .... 45 minutes to get to the airport.

   Ⓐ have   Ⓑ get   Ⓒ take

........3. You should .... your fear of water.

   Ⓐ get over   Ⓑ get alone   Ⓒ get off

........4. Would you like to .... a swim this afternoon?

   Ⓐ go   Ⓑ go for   Ⓒ go on

........5. The festival will .... in Shanghai next month.

   Ⓐ take place   Ⓑ get together   Ⓒ have fun

........6. I'll .... your advice and give it another try.

   Ⓐ get   Ⓑ take   Ⓒ have

........7. The plane is going to .... in fifteen minutes. Please fasten your seatbelts.

   Ⓐ take place   Ⓑ take off   Ⓒ take over

........8. Father .... a business trip to Hong Kong.

   Ⓐ has made   Ⓑ has gone for   Ⓒ has gone on

........9. Why don't you .... his job offer?

   Ⓐ do   Ⓑ make   Ⓒ take

........10. What's .... here?

   Ⓐ going on   Ⓑ getting on   Ⓒ taking off

........11. The teacher wants us to ....

   Ⓐ do a favor   Ⓑ do our good   Ⓒ do our best

........12. He is a weird guy. I can't .... with him at all.

   Ⓐ get over   Ⓑ get together   Ⓒ get along

........13. The shirt is .... 100% cotton.

   Ⓐ made of   Ⓑ made from   Ⓒ made on

........14. This matter .... Jenny.

   Ⓐ doesn't have something to do with

   Ⓑ has anything to do with

   Ⓒ has nothing to do with

2 看圖自表中選出正確的片語，以正確的形式填空。

→ **Unit 50-53 重點複習**

is made of
is made from
go for
go on
get along
get over
take part in
take place

1. Cheese _____ milk.

2. My parents and I _____ a walk this afternoon.

3. Lucky and Puffy cannot _____ with each other.

4. Jessica _____ the play last week.

5. My family decided to _____ a vacation in Europe.

6. The music festival _____ in August, 2008.

7. _____ your fear and try parachuting.

8. This vase _____ glass.

3 將括弧內的動詞以正確形式填空。
→ Unit 56–58 重點複習

1. My brother made me _____ (finish) all the leftovers on the table.

2. Could you please get somebody _____ (change) the sheets and pillowcases?

3. Will you have everything _____ (finish) in twenty minutes?

4. Father had me _____ (clean) the bathroom on Sunday.

5. I'll have David _____ (apologize) to you.

6. The boss had everyone _____ (work) overtime last weekend.

7. I just want to get things _____ (do) as soon as possible.

8. Jason had his house _____ (paint) .

9. Please get someone _____ (remove) the stain on the wall.

10. I'll have him _____ (explain) to you in person.

11. I'll get my bicycle _____ (repair) tomorrow.

4 在問句的空格內填上正確的動詞,並依據事實,用完整的句子回答問題。
→ Unit 50–53 重點複習

1. Did you _____ your hair cut last week?

→ _____

2. Do you have to _____ a lot of homework tonight?

→ _____

3. Does your family _____ on a picnic every weekend?

→ _____

4. Do you like to _____ pictures of dogs and cats?

→ _____

5. Do you _____ care of your little sister when your parents are out?

→ _____

6. Do you like to _____ camping on your summer vacation?

→ _____

7. Do you _____ the dishes every day?

→ _____

8. Do you .... a shower in the morning?

→ ....

9. Do you .... crazy with your homework every day?

→ ....

10. Do you .... a lot of mistakes?

→ ....

11. Have you ever .... the dentist fill a cavity?

→ ....

5 將下列圖中所代表的名詞，依據其前面該用的動詞，填到正確的框內。
→ Unit 51-52 重點複習

1 ▶ do	2 ▶ take	3 ▶ make
exercise		
....	....	....
....	....	....

a nap

exercise

friends

the laundry

a bath

a wish

a break

money

the shopping

Part 8 Modal Verbs 情態助動詞

Unit 60

Can
Can 的用法

1 情態助動詞是與另一個動詞連用，**表達特定意義的**動詞。
主詞不分人稱、單複數，情態助動詞的形式都只有一種。

常見的情態助動詞有：

- can
- may
- must
- should
- could
- might
- would
- shall

2 can 是情態助動詞，後面只能接**動詞原形**，通常用來表示「**能力**」，此時用於現在式。

Buddy can run really fast.
巴弟可以跑得很快。

My dog can shake hands.
我的狗會握手。

Willy can dance, but he can't sing.
威利會跳舞，但不會唱歌。

He can play basketball. 他會打籃球。

3 can 也可以用來表「**可能性**」。

I can meet you after 4:00 this afternoon.
我今天下午 4 點以後可以跟你碰面。

The director can see you next Tuesday.
主任下星期二可以見你。

否定句的全形和縮寫	
I cannot play	I can't play
you cannot play	you can't play
he cannot play	he can't play
she cannot play	she can't play
it cannot play	it can't play
we cannot play	we can't play
they cannot play	they can't play

疑問句的句型	
Can I play?	Can it play?
Can you play?	Can we play?
Can he play?	Can they play?
Can she play?	

肯定和否定的簡答	
Yes, I can.	No, I can't.
Yes, you can.	No, you can't.
Yes, he can.	No, he can't.
Yes, she can.	No, she can't.
Yes, it can.	No, it can't.
Yes, we can.	No, we can't.
Yes, they can.	No, they can't.

4 在情態助動詞的後面加上 not，可以構成**否定句**。
can 較為特別，它的否定形式是 cannot（連在一起寫），常縮寫為 can't，用來表示「不能」或「不允許」。

I can't speak French. 我不會說法文。

You cannot enter that room.
你不可以進那個房間。

5 情態助動詞的**疑問句**，是把情態助動詞移到句首。所以**把 can 移到句首**，就構成了**疑問句**。

Can you play the piano? 你會彈鋼琴嗎？

Can we park our car here?
我們可以把車停在這裡嗎？

Practice

1

在各個圖示中，Ⓨ 表示 Chris 會演奏這種樂器，Ⓝ 表示他不會。
用 can 或 can't 造句，描述 Chris 會的樂器和不會的樂器。
左方列表有提示的樂器名稱。

flute
violin
guitar
piano
drums
saxophone

1. *Chris can play the guitar.*
2. _____
3. _____
4. _____
5. _____
6. _____

2

依據事實，用 can 或
can't 回答問題。

1. Can you speak English?
   → *Yes, I can. I can speak English.*
2. Can you read German?
   → _____
3. Can you hang out with your friends on the weekend?
   → _____
4. Can you run very fast?
   → _____
5. Can your mother cook Mexican food?
   → _____
6. Can a dog fly?
   → _____
7. Can a pig climb a tree?
   → _____
8. Can we speak loudly in the museum?
   → _____

Unit 61

Could
Could 的用法

否定句的全形和縮寫	
I could not speak	I couldn't speak
you could not speak	you couldn't speak
he could not speak	he couldn't speak
she could not speak	she couldn't speak
it could not speak	it couldn't speak
we could not speak	we couldn't speak
they could not speak	they couldn't speak

疑問句的句型	
Could I speak?	Could it speak?
Could you speak?	Could we speak?
Could he speak?	Could they speak?
Could she speak?	

肯定和否定的簡答	
Yes, I could.	No, I couldn't.
Yes, you could.	No, you couldn't.
Yes, he could.	No, he couldn't.
Yes, she could.	No, she couldn't.
Yes, it could.	No, it couldn't.
Yes, we could.	No, we couldn't.
Yes, they could.	No, they couldn't.

1 could 也是情態助動詞，後面要**接動詞原形**，用來表示「**過去的能力**」。在表示這種意義的時候，常被視為是 can 的過去式。

He <u>could</u> <u>read</u> Japanese when he was five.
他五歲就看得懂日語。

He <u>could</u> <u>speak</u> five languages by the time he graduated from high school.
他高中畢業的時候，就會說五種語言了。

2 could 的疑問句型，是將 could 移至句首。

Could he <u>speak</u> Farsi before he went to Iran? 他在去伊朗之前，就會說波斯話了嗎？

Could you please <u>be</u> quiet?
麻煩你安靜一點好嗎？

3 could 也可以用於現在式，表示「**請求幫助**」，語氣比 can 更有禮貌。

Could you please <u>help</u> me?
↳ 用 could 較為正式、禮貌
請問你能幫我個忙嗎？

Can you <u>give</u> me a hand?
↳ 用 can 較不正式
你可以幫我個忙嗎？

4 could 的否定形態是 **could not**，縮寫為 **couldn't**。

Peter <u>couldn't</u> <u>skate</u> before he met Jane.
彼德在認識珍之前並不會溜冰。

I <u>couldn't</u> <u>speak</u> when I saw him arrive.
I just cried with joy.
當我看到他來時，我喜極而泣，高興得說不出話。

Practice

1

請依圖示，自右表選出正確的片語，用 could 的句型填空。

make pots	paint landscapes
sculpt figures	shoot photographs
write calligraphy	paint pictures

1

Lucy ....
....
when she was 10 years old.

2

Johnny ....
....
when he was 5 years old.

3

Sandra ....
.... when
she was 15 years old.

4

Kelly ....
.... when
she was 10 years old.

5

Laura ....
....
when she was 65 years old.

6

Jane ....
....
when she was 18 years old.

2

當你 12 歲的時候，你已經會做哪些事？還不會做哪些事？

請依據事實，用 could 的肯定或否定句型，寫出完整句子回答問題。

1. Could you play the piano when you were twelve?
   → ....

2. Could you swim when you were twelve?
   → ....

3. Could you use a computer when you were twelve?
   → ....

4. Could you read novels in English when you were twelve?
   → ....

5. Could you ride a bicycle when you were twelve?
   → ....

Part 8 Modal Verbs 情態助動詞

Unit 62

Must
Must 的用法

1 must 是**情態助動詞**，用來表示「**必要性**」或「**義務**」，後面要接**動詞原形**。

> **Drill Sergeant** Every day you <u>must</u> get up at 5:30 a.m. Every day you <u>must</u> run 10 kilometers and then <u>must</u> do 100 sit-ups and 150 push-ups.
>
> **軍隊士官長** 你們每天早上要五點半起床，先跑 10 公里，再做 100 下的仰臥起坐和 150 下伏地挺身。

My passport is about to expire. I <u>must</u> renew my passport.

我的護照快要過期了，我必須更換新護照。

I have a problem with my tooth. I <u>must</u> go to the dentist tomorrow.

我的牙齒有毛病，我明天得去看牙醫。

2 must 也可表示「**極有可能**」，具有「**一定是**」、「**一定要**」的意思。但要注意這種用法的 must 只能用於**肯定句**。

You <u>must</u> be Mrs. Smith. Your daughter has told me many good things about you.

妳一定是史密斯太太，妳女兒跟我提起很多關於妳的好事。

否定用法時

如果要表達否定意義「**極不可能**」，或疑問意義「**有可能嗎**」則必須用 can。

- He <u>can't</u> be at his office. I saw him in the grocery store just ten minutes ago.

  他不可能在辦公室呀，因為我十分鐘前才在雜貨店看到他。

- <u>Can</u> it <u>be</u> Jessica at the door?

  門外會是潔西卡嗎？

否定句的全形和縮寫	
I must not use	I mustn't use
you must not use	you mustn't use
he must not use	he mustn't use
she must not use	she mustn't use
it must not use	it mustn't use
we must not use	we mustn't use
they must not use	they mustn't use

疑問句的句型	
Must I use . . . ?	Must it use . . . ?
Must you use . . . ?	Must we use . . . ?
Must he use . . . ?	Must they use . . . ?
Must she use . . . ?	

肯定和否定的簡答	
Yes, I must.	No, I mustn't.
Yes, you must.	No, you mustn't.
Yes, he must.	No, he mustn't.
Yes, she must.	No, she mustn't.
Yes, it must.	No, it mustn't.
Yes, we must.	No, we mustn't.
Yes, they must.	No, they mustn't.

3 must 的否定句型是 must not，縮寫為 mustn't，用來表示「**禁止**」。

You <u>must not</u> miss the Autumn Festival.

你不可以錯過秋季嘉年華。

You <u>mustn't</u> forget your mother's birthday.

你不可以忘記你媽媽的生日。

You <u>mustn't</u> touch the wall before the paint dries.

在油漆乾掉以前，絕不能碰牆壁。

4 must 本身不使用於過去式，如果要表達過去必須做的事，請用 had to 來代替。

As a child growing up on a farm, I had to milk the cows every morning.

身為農場長大的小孩，我以前每天早上都得擠牛奶。

Practice

1

哪些是該做或不該做的事？請將括弧內的動詞以 must、mustn't 或 had to 的句型來填空。

1. You _____ (finish) your homework before watching TV.

2. You _____ (smoke) cigarettes.

3. We _____ (clean) the house before the party started.

4. You _____ (fight) with your sisters or brothers.

5. Tell Billy that he _____ (come) home before dinner.

6. You _____ (finish) your dinner before eating dessert.

7. Tony forgot to bring his keys, so he _____ (break) the window to get into the house.

8. You _____ (eat) too much fast food.

9. Marie _____ (behave) herself at school.

10. I overslept yesterday so I _____ (run) to catch the bus.

2

自下表選出適當詞彙，用 must 或 mustn't 的句型回應各個句子。

lose it
hurry
go to bed
be careful
eat something
fight with them
drink something

1. I'm late.
   → *You must hurry.*

2. I'm very tired.
   → _____

3. I'm starving.
   → _____

4. I'm extremely dehydrated.
   → _____

5. I'm cutting glass all day.
   → _____

6. I'm having a fight with my parents.
   → _____

7. I'm carrying a large amount of money in my wallet.
   → _____

Unit 63

Have to
Have to 的用法

1 have to 不是情態助動詞，但它的意義和 must 相同，常用來表示「**必要性**」和「**義務**」。

You have to **take out the garbage.**
你必須把垃圾拿出去丟。

Young adult males have to **serve in the military for one year.**
年輕的成年男子必須當一年兵。

You have to **pay the phone bill.**
你必須付電話帳單。

2 have to 的否定句型是 don't have to 或 doesn't have to，表示「**不需要做某些事**」。

We don't have to **do any homework tonight.**
我們今晚完全不用做功課。

Jim doesn't have to **go to his office today.**
吉姆今天不用去上班。

You don't have to **return his call.**
你不需要回他電話。

3 have to 的疑問句型，是在句首加上 **Do** 或 **Does**。

Do we have to **come home so early?**
我們一定要這麼早回家嗎？

Does Helen have to **cook dinner every day?**
海倫每天都必須做晚餐嗎？

肯定句的句型	
I have to cook	it has to cook
you have to cook	we have to cook
he has to cook	they have to cook
she has to cook	

否定句的全形和縮寫	
I do not have to cook	I don't have to cook
you do not have to cook	you don't have to cook
he does not have to cook	he doesn't have to cook
she does not have to cook	she doesn't have to cook
it does not have to cook	it doesn't have to cook
we do not have to cook	we don't have to cook
they do not have to cook	they don't have to cook

疑問句的句型	
Do I have to cook . . . ?	Does it have to cook . . . ?
Do you have to cook . . . ?	Do we have to cook . . . ?
Does he have to cook . . . ?	Do they have to cook . . . ?
Does she have to cook . . . ?	

肯定和否定的簡答	
Yes, I do.	No, I don't.
Yes, you do.	No, you don't.
Yes, he does.	No, he doesn't.
Yes, she does.	No, she doesn't.
Yes, it does.	No, it doesn't.
Yes, we do.	No, we don't.
Yes, they do.	No, they don't.

Practice

1 自下表選出與圖片相符的片語，用 have to 或 has to 的句型描述圖中這些辦公室職員每天必須做的事。

pack products	make copies
answer the phone	work on the computer

She has to pack products.

2

通常主管不需要自己做哪些事呢？

請依提示，用 don't have to 或 doesn't have to 描述這些事。

deliver the mail

make coffee

show up every day

fax documents

1. Judy _____

2. Mr. Taylor and Mr. Watson _____

3. James _____

4. Ms. Keaton _____

Unit 64

Comparison Between "Must" and "Have to"
Must 和 Have to 的比較

1 have to 的過去式是 **had to**，
表示過去必須做某件事。
had to 也被用作 must 的過去式。

I had to walk thirty minutes to school when I was a child.
我小的時候，都要走 30 分鐘的路去上學。

2 have to 過去式的否定句型是：
did not have to 或 **didn't have to**。

I did not have to do the dishes last night because it was Jerry's turn.
昨晚我不用洗碗，因為輪到傑瑞洗了。

I didn't have to go to school last Friday because of a typhoon.
上個星期五因為有颱風，我不用去上學。

3 have to 過去式的疑問句型是：
Did . . . have to . . . ?

Did you have to pass the Red Cross life saving test to become a lifeguard?
你要先通過紅十字會的救生測驗，才能成為救生員嗎？

I had to pass the life saving test to become a lifeguard.
為了當救生員，我們要通過救生測驗。

He didn't have to pass the life saving test because he decided not to become a lifeguard.
他不必通過救生測驗，因為他決定不當救生員。

4 在肯定句型裡，have to 的語氣比 must 強烈。
must 只是表達個人的要求或意見，
have to 則有必須強制執行的意味。

You must eat all your vegetables.
↳ 我覺得你應該要把青菜吃完。
你必須把所有的青菜吃完。

You have to pay the tax. 你一定要繳稅。
↳ 法律規定

You have to hand in your homework tomorrow. 你們明天一定要把作業交出來。
↳ 學校規定

5 在否定句型裡，mustn't 的語氣比 don't have to 或 doesn't have to 強烈，意思也不同。mustn't 指「不可以做某件事」，don't have to 指「不需要做某件事」。

You mustn't walk yet.
你還不可以走路。

You don't have to put sugar in that coffee.
↳ 可能是已經很甜了，不需要再加糖。
你不用在那杯咖啡裡加糖。

Practice

1

說說看，你上個星期有哪些必須做的事？又有哪些不必做的事？

用 had to 或 didn't have to 來造句。

1. I had to go to school from Monday to Friday.
2. ....
3. ....
4. ....
5. ....
6. ....

2

根據圖示中的標示，並利用括弧提供的動詞或片語，用下面的句型造句：

• You mustn't . . .
• You don't have to . . .

1. ....

   (smoke) in the café.

2. ....

   (pay cash) in this shop.

3. ....

   (skateboard) in the park.

4. ....

   (talk on a cell phone) in the movie theater.

5. ....

   (pay full price) during a sale.

Unit 65

May and Might
May 和 Might 的用法

1 may 和 might 是**情態助動詞**，後面要接**動詞原形**，用來表示「**可能性**」或「**可能會發生的事**」。

We <u>may upgrade</u> the operating system on the computer.
我們可能會將這台電腦的作業系統升級。

We <u>might buy</u> a new computer game.
我們可能會買個新的電腦遊戲。

2 may 和 might 的差別不大，都是指「**未來可能會發生的事**」，但是 might 發生的可能性比 may 稍微少一點。

I <u>may order</u> a pepperoni pizza.
我可能會叫個義式香腸披薩。

I <u>may go</u> to my mother's house for dinner.
我可能會去我媽家吃晚餐。

I <u>might</u> even <u>cook</u> something myself, but I doubt it.
我甚至可能自己煮東西來吃，不過關於這點我很懷疑。

否定句的句型	
I may not leave	I might not leave
you may not leave	you might not leave
he may not leave	he might not leave
she may not leave	she might not leave
it may not leave	it might not leave
we may not leave	we might not leave
they may not leave	they might not leave

3 might 可被視為是 may 的過去式，如果是**表示過去事件的可能性**，則要使用 might，常用於**間接引語**中。

Father said he <u>might go</u> to Hong Kong for business. 父親說他可能會去香港洽商。

Liz said she <u>might go</u> to a movie with Jason the next day.
麗茲說她隔天可能會和傑森去看電影。

4 may 和 might 表示「**可能性**」的時候，通常**不會用於疑問句**。

✗ May you come shopping with us this afternoon?

✗ Might you go to visit your cousin this evening?

5 may 和 might 也可以用來**請求許可**，這個時候**使用 might 又更為客氣**。

Pardon me. <u>May I borrow</u> your cart?
I need to move some computer equipment.
不好意思，我可以借你的推車嗎？我需要搬一些電腦設備。

<u>Might I ask</u> you a question?
　　↳ 更客氣
我可以請教您一個問題嗎？

Practice

1

自下表選出適當的動詞片語，自由以 may 或 might 的句型填空。

win the set （贏下這局）

win the race （贏得賽事）

clear the bar （跳過這一桿）

hit a home run （擊出全壘打）

block the shot （守住對方射門）

score a touchdown （達陣）

This goalie ___may___ ___block the shot___ .

This batter _____ _____ .

This tennis player _____ _____ .

This football player _____ _____ .

Horse No. 3 _____ _____ .

This pole vaulter _____ _____ .

2

利用括弧裡的 may 或 might 改寫句子。

1. Perhaps we will go to the seashore tomorrow. (may)
→ _____

2. Perhaps I will take you on a trip to visit my hometown. (might)
→ _____

3. Maybe we can pick up Grandpa on the way. (may)
→ _____

4. Perhaps we can visit my sister in Sydney next year. (might)
→ _____

5. Perhaps my sister will bring her husband and baby to visit us instead. (may)
→ _____

6. Maybe we can go to Hong Kong for the weekend. (might)
→ _____

7. Perhaps you will go to a boarding school in Switzerland. (may)
→ _____

8. Or maybe you will go to live with your grandparents. (might)
→ _____

Unit **66**

Should
Should 的用法

否定句的全形和縮寫	
I should not talk	I shouldn't talk
you should not talk	you shouldn't talk
he should not talk	he shouldn't talk
she should not talk	she shouldn't talk
it should not talk	it shouldn't talk
we should not talk	we shouldn't talk
they should not talk	they shouldn't talk

1 should 是**情態助動詞**，後面要接**動詞原形**，可以用來**提供意見**。

You should use deodorant.
你應該要用體香劑。

Your hair looks funny. You should wash it or get a haircut.
你的頭髮看起來很好笑，你應該要洗一洗或剪個頭髮。

2 should 也可以指「**我們認為正確的事**」或「**希望別人去做的事**」。

The government should ease immigration restrictions. 政府應當要減少移民的限制。

Laid-off workers should be given free classes to train them for new jobs.
應該要為那些被解僱的員工們，開辦輔導他們重新就業的免費課程。

3 should 可表示「**現在**」或「**未來**」。

現在 I should go now or I will be late.
我得走了，否則我會遲到。

未來 I should depart after the next song.
下一首歌結束後，我就該走了。

現在 You should leave now or you will miss the bus.
你現在就應該出發，否則你會錯過公車。

4 should 常用在以下句型：
　・I think you should . . .
　・I don't think you should . . .

I don't think you should have any more alcohol.
我想你不應該再喝酒了。

I don't think you should drive and drink.
我認為你不該酒後駕車。

5 should 的疑問句，經常使用「do you think I should . . .」。

Why do you think you should be driving your car on the sidewalk?
你為什麼認為可以在人行道上開車？

Do you think Jessica should go to medical school? 你覺得潔西卡應該去念醫學院嗎？

肯定和否定的簡答	
Yes, I should.	No, I shouldn't.
Yes, you should.	No, you shouldn't.
Yes, he should.	No, he shouldn't.
Yes, she should.	No, she shouldn't.
Yes, it should.	No, it shouldn't.
Yes, we should.	No, we shouldn't.
Yes, they should.	No, they shouldn't.

Practice

1

自下表選用適當的動詞，分別以 should 和 shouldn't 造句。

arrive
work
eat
yield
feed
take
cheat
respect

1. We _____ on a subway train.
2. We _____ seats to the elderly on a subway train.

3. Students _____ on an exam.
4. Students _____ their teachers and themselves.

5. You _____ late.
6. You _____ hard.

7. You _____ your dog French fries.
8. You _____ your dog out for a run.

2

利用題目提供的詞彙，分別用下面的句型造句：
• Should . . . ?
• Do you think . . . should . . . ?

1. I | call the director about the résumé I sent
   → *Should I call the director about the résumé I sent?*
   → *Do you think I should call the director about the résumé I sent?*

2. I | bring a gift with me
   → _____
   → _____

3. Mike | go on a vacation once in a while
   → _____
   → _____

4. we | visit our grandma more often
   → _____
   → _____

5. I | ask Nancy out for a date
   → _____
   → _____

6. Sally | apply for that job in the restaurant
   → _____
   → _____

Unit **67**

Requests : May, Could, Can
表示請求的用語：May、Could、Can

1 may、can、could 都可以用來表示**請求**。

<u>May I</u> please see the latest sales report?
請問我可以看最新的銷售報表嗎？

<u>May I</u> have a cookie and a glass of milk?
我可以要一片餅乾和一杯牛奶嗎？

<u>Could you</u> turn on the light so I can see it better?
可以請你把燈打開嗎？這樣我才可以看得更清楚。

<u>Could I</u> open this package and see what's inside?
我可以拆開包裝，看看裡面是什麼嗎？

<u>Can I</u> sit down at your desk while I read the newspaper?
我在看報紙的時候，可以坐在你的座位上嗎？

<u>Can you</u> run to the store and get some soy milk?
你可以跑去商店買一些豆漿嗎？

2 語氣上，may 比 could 和 can 更正式，而 could 又比 can 更禮貌。

最正式	<u>May I</u> please have another waffle?
禮貌，但不正式	<u>Could I</u> please have another waffle?
不正式	<u>Can I</u> have another waffle?
沒禮貌	Give me another waffle.

<u>May I</u> serve the wine now?
請問可以上酒了嗎？

3 may、can、could 常拿來表示「請求允許做某件事」。

If nobody is going to eat it, <u>may</u> I have the last piece of cake?
如果沒有人要吃，我可以吃這最後一塊蛋糕嗎？

<u>Could I</u> finish the grapes?
我可以把葡萄吃光嗎？

<u>Can I</u> put my feet up while I digest all the food I just ate?
我剛吃的食物還在肚裡沒消化完，我可以休息一下嗎？

4 could 和 can 可用來「請求他人幫忙」；may 則不能這麼用。

<u>Could you</u> help me with this test?
你可以幫我做這題測驗嗎？

<u>Can you</u> introduce me to her?
你能介紹我認識她嗎？

Practice

1

服飾店裡有名男子正在挑選衣物，請按物品編號，依序寫出他會問的問題。從右表挑選適當的詞彙，並用下面的句型造句：

- May I . . . ?
- Could I . . . ?
- Can I . . . ?

pay with a credit card

get two more shirts just like this one

have three pairs of socks similar to these

have a tie that goes with my shirt

1. → May I get two more shirts just like this one?

 → Could I get two more shirts just like this one?

 → Can I get two more shirts just like this one?

2. →

 →

 →

3. →

 →

 →

4. →

 →

 →

2

自右表選出正確的用語，以提示的「情態助動詞」造句完成對話。

speak to Dennis   turn up the heat

borrow your father's drill   put my files here

move these boxes for me

1. _____ (may)

 Hang on, please. I'll get him on the phone.

2. _____ (may)

 I'm not sure. I'll ask him about it.

3. _____ (could)

 I'm sorry, but I think they're too heavy for me, too.

4. _____ (could)

 No problem. Is it warmer now?

5. _____ (can)

 Yes, of course. That shelf belongs to you.

Unit 68

Offers and Invitations：Would Like, Will, Shall

表示提供和邀請的用語：
Would Like、Will、Shall

1
「Would you like + 名詞？」
用來表「**提供對方某樣東西**」。

Would you like a vacation in Rome?
你想要去羅馬度個假嗎？

Would you like a free trip to Japan?
你想要免費的日本旅遊嗎？

1
_____ some more tea?
你要不要再來一點茶？

2
「Would you like + 帶 to 的不定詞？」
用來表「**邀請對方做某件事**」。

Would you like to take a look at this video about the moon?
你想不想看這部關於月亮的影片？

Would you like to go some place warm and sunny?
你想不想到一個溫暖且充滿陽光的地方去？

Would you like to visit a tropical paradise?
你想不想參觀一個熱帶天堂？

2
_____ to a movie with me?
你要不要和我去看電影？

3
「Would you like me + 帶 to 的不定詞」用來表示「**提供對方某種服務**」。

Would you like me to mail that letter for you?
要我幫你寄那封信嗎？

Would you like me to buy you a lottery ticket?
要我幫你買張樂透彩券嗎？

3
_____ that box for you?
你要我幫你打開那個盒子嗎？

4
「I will + 動詞原形」用來表「**願意幫忙做某件事**」，可縮寫成「I'll + 動詞原形」。

I'll do it. 我願意去做這件事。

I'll carry that box for you.
我會幫你提那個箱子。

I'll run out and buy you some ice cream .
我願意跑一趟，幫你買一些冰淇淋。

5
「Shall I + 動詞原形」這個句型的意思等於「Do you want me to . . . ?」，用來表「**提供對方某種幫助**」。

Shall I walk you out to your car?
要不要我陪你走去車子那裡？

Shall I call next week and see if you are free?
我下星期打給你，到時再看你有沒有空好嗎？

4
_____ the curtain for you?
我幫你把窗簾拉下來好嗎？

Practice

Would you like + 名詞 . . . ?　　I'll . . .

Would you like me to . . . ?　　Shall I . . . ?

1

依照範例，利用題目提示的詞彙，分別用表中的四種句型，造出表示提供某樣東西的問句。

1. make some fruit salad
   → *Would you like some fruit salad?*
   → *Would you like me to make some fruit salad?*
   → *I'll make some fruit salad for you.*
   → *Shall I make some fruit salad for you?*

2. make some tea
   →
   →
   →
   →

3. squeeze some orange juice
   →
   →
   →
   →

4. make some pudding
   →
   →
   →
   →

2

依據圖示，自下表選出正確的片語，以「Would you like to . . . ?」的句型完成句子。

go hiking

go fishing

go to the beach

play basketball

have some pizza

1　*Would you like to go* *fishing* this Saturday?

2　_____ tomorrow?

3　_____ on Sunday?

4　_____ next Tuesday?

5　_____ for lunch?

49

Unit **69**

Suggestions: Shall We, What Shall We, Why Don't We, Let's, How About

表示提議的用語：Shall We、What Shall We、Why Don't We、Let's、How About

1 「Shall we . . .」用來表示「**提議**」，後面要接**動詞原形**。

Shall we **go see** Steven in the hospital?
我們要不要到醫院去看史蒂芬？

Shall we **help** your father paint the garage? 我們要不要幫你爸爸油漆車庫？

Shall we **join** a study abroad tour?
我們去參加遊學之旅好不好？

2 要「**詢問意見**」，則可以用**疑問詞**（what、where、when 等）搭配 shall we。

What shall we **do** today?
= What should we **do** today?
我們今天要做什麼？（美式較常用 should）

Where shall we **meet** Ken and Gina?
我們要在哪裡跟肯和吉娜碰面？

When shall we **invite** them over?
我們什麼時候要邀請他們過來？

1 _____ during summer vacation? 我們暑假期間要做些什麼？

3 「Let's (= Let us) + **動詞原形**」也常用表示「**提議**」，通常用於**肯定句**。

Let's **visit** our high school math teacher, Mr. Chen.
我們一起去拜訪高中數學的陳老師吧。

Let's **go** to Canada. 我們去加拿大吧。

Let's **stay** up all night and see the sunrise.
我們來熬夜看日出吧。

4 「Why don't we . . .」也用來表達「**提議**」，後面要接**動詞原形**。

Why don't we **take** a road trip?
我們何不來趟公路之旅？

Why don't we **volunteer** at the library on Saturdays?
我們要不要每星期六都去圖書當義工？

Why don't we **visit** the Canadian Rockies after the tour?
我們何不在這次旅行之後，去參觀加拿大洛磯山脈？

5 How about 也表示「**提議**」，後面要接**動名詞**（V-ing）或是**名詞**。

How about **visiting** the old neighborhood?
我們去拜訪一下老鄰居如何？

How about **calling** Jimmy to see if he is free?
我們何不打個電話給吉米看他有沒有空？

How about **a walk** in the park?
到公園去散個步如何？

How about **a trip** to the mall?
你覺得到購物中心如何？

2 _____ Yellowknife and hunting moose? 你覺得到黃刀鎮去獵麋鹿怎麼樣？

Practice

1

依照範例，利用各題目提示的動詞，
分別用右表的四種句型造句。

Shall we . . . ?

Why don't we . . . ?

How about . . . ?

Let's . . . .

1. play another volleyball game

   → ....
   → ....
   → ....
   → ....

2. go on a picnic

   → ....
   → ....
   → ....
   → ....

3. eat out tonight

   → ....
   → ....
   → ....
   → ....

4. take a walk

   → ....
   → ....
   → ....
   → ....

5. go to Bali this summer

   → ....
   → ....
   → ....
   → ....

6. have Chinese food for dinner

   → ....
   → ....
   → ....
   → ....

Part 8

Unit 70
Review Test of Units 60–69
單元 60–69 總複習

1 依據圖示，自下方表中選出正確的動詞，用 can 寫出問句，詢問是否會烹調圖中的食物。依據實際情況做出簡答後，再以完整句子描述事實。

→ Unit 60 重點複習

tea eggs

tomatoes

French fries

hamburgers

muffins

coffee

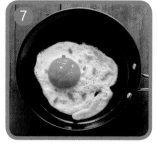
an egg

a bun

fry 油煎
make 泡
bake 烘烤
purée 製漿
boil 水煮
deep fry 油炸
grill 燒烤
steam 蒸

1. Q *Can you boil tea eggs?*
   A *No, I can't. I can't boil tea eggs.*
2. Q
   A
3. Q
   A
4. Q
   A
5. Q
   A
6. Q
   A
7. Q
   A
8. Q
   A

2 請用「do . . . have to」或「does . . . have to」填空完成下列問句。
→ Unit 63 重點複習

1. How old _____ you _____ be to get a motorcycle driver's license?

2. _____ every person in a car _____ wear a seatbelt?

3. _____ you _____ take a written test and a road test to get an automobile driver's license?

4. _____ you _____ pass an entrance exam to go to college?

5. _____ every adult citizen _____ pay income tax?

6. How old _____ you _____ be to vote for the President?

3 自下表選出適當的句型來完成下列餐廳與飯店內的對話，並且注意要用禮貌的語氣。
→ Unit 60–68 重點複習

| Can I |
| May I |
| I'll |
| Could you |
| Shall I |
| How about |
| Would you |

1. Waiter : _____ take your order?

   Guest : Yes, I'll have a fish fillet and a bowl of onion soup.

2. Guest : _____ have the table by the window?

   Waiter : I'm afraid it's reserved.

3. Guest : _____ send someone to fix the towel rod in my

   bathroom?

   Receptionist : I'll send someone up right away.

4. Guest : It's a little stuffy in the room.

   Bellboy : _____ turn on the air conditioner for you?

5. Waiter : _____ like a tomato salad or a chicken salad?

   Guest : A chicken salad, please.

6. Guest : I didn't order fruit tea. I ordered a pot of milk tea.

   Waiter : I'm terribly sorry. _____ bring your milk tea right away.

7. Guest : I want to have something light.

   Waiter : _____ the chicken soup? It's popular among our guests.

8. Guest : I don't like chicken. Do you have anything else?

   Waiter : _____ like to try Today's Special? It's steamed fish. It's

   a light dish, too.

4 從圖中選出適當的詞彙，用「Would you like ...?」的句型造問句，完成下列空服員（**F** Flight Attendant）與乘客（**P** Passenger）間的對話。

→ Unit 68 重點複習

1. **F** *Would you like something to drink?*

   P Yes, please. What do you have?

2. **F** _____

   P No, thanks. I don't drink beer or wine.

3. **F** _____

   P No, thanks. It's too sweet. Do you have anything hot?

4. **F** _____

   P A cup of tea would be great.

5. **F** _____

   P No, thank you. I'm not hungry.

   F Enjoy your tea.

a bag of nuts

some juice

a cup of coffee or tea

an alcoholic beverage

something to drink

5 將下列句子改寫為否定句。

→ Unit 60–66 重點複習

My dog can sing! → *My dog can't sing.*

1. I can walk to work.

   → _____

2. Susie could dance all night.

   → _____

3. I have to go to Joe's house tonight.

   → _____

4. I have to go to see the doctor tomorrow.

   → _____

5. I may go on a vacation in August.

   → _____

6. I might go see the Picasso exhibit at the museum.

   → _____

7. My friend can sit in the full lotus position.

→ ....

8. I can finish all my homework this weekend.

→ ....

9. I must stop eating beans.

→ ....

10. John has to see Joseph.

→ ....

11. The turtle may win the race against the rabbit.

→ ....

12. My friend Jon should get a different job.

→ ....

6 將下列句子改寫為疑問句。
→ Unit 60–66 重點複習

1. You can fry an egg.

→ *Can you fry an egg?* ....

2. Paul could swim out to the island.

→ ....

3. John must go to Japan.

→ ....

4. Abby has to go to the studio.

→ ....

5. George can play the guitar.

→ ....

6. David must finish his homework before he goes outside to play.

→ ....

7. They have to cross the road.

→ ....

8. I have to give away my concert tickets.

→ ....

9. Joan has to stay at home tomorrow night.

→ ....

.... 1. Bob : I'm bored. _____ go somewhere?

Ⓐ Why don't we   Ⓑ Shall we   Ⓒ Both A and B

.... 2. Stan : _____ taking a ride on the subway?

Ⓐ How about   Ⓑ Why don't we   Ⓒ Shall we

.... 3. Bob : Great. _____ go.

Ⓐ Why don't we   Ⓑ Shall we   Ⓒ Let's

.... 4. Stan : _____ go to Forest Park?

Ⓐ Shall we   Ⓑ How about   Ⓒ Let's

.... 5. Bob : _____ do at Forest Park?

Ⓐ What shall we   Ⓑ Shall we   Ⓒ Both A and B

.... 6. Stan : _____ taking a walk in the park?

Bob : No. That's boring.

Ⓐ How about   Ⓑ Shall we   Ⓒ Let's

.... 7. Stan : In that case, _____ do?

Bob : I want to go home and watch TV.

Ⓐ what shall we   Ⓑ let's   Ⓒ why don't we

.... 8. Stan : _____ forget about it. You go home.

I'm going for a walk in the park.

Ⓐ How about   Ⓑ Shall we   Ⓒ Let's

.... 9. Stan : OK. _____ take a walk in Forest Park.

Ⓐ How about   Ⓑ Let's   Ⓒ Why don't we

.... 10. Stan : _____ hop the next train?

Ⓐ Let's   Ⓑ Shall we   Ⓒ What shall we

8 請將各個句子依據情態助動詞的作用，填入適當的分類編號。
→ Unit 59–69 重點複習

A

Asking for something
請求得到某物

B

Asking permission
請求允許

C

Asking someone to do something 請求他人幫忙

D

Offering something
供應物品

E

Inviting someone
邀請他人

F

Offering to do something
願意幫忙做某事

G

Asking for a suggestion
徵求意見

H

Making a suggestion
提議

1. Can I have a cookie, please?

2. Would you like one more croissant?

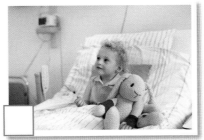

3. Why don't we visit Sam tomorrow?

4. Can you call the police for me?

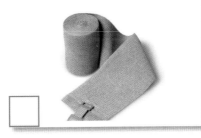

5. I'll go get a bandage for you.

6. May I try on this shirt?

7. What should I do with my parents?

8. Would you like to play badminton?

9 依據對話的意思，用 must 或 mustn't 搭配括弧中的動詞完成對話。
→ Unit 62 重點複習

1. Jack： Susan has been working for six hours.

   Olive： She _____ (be) very tired. She should take a break.

2. Eddie： Ken has gone to Japan for a vacation. It's his mother's birthday today.

   Yvonne： His mother says he _____ (visit) her in Tokyo.

3. Ada： Bob hasn't eaten anything the whole day.

   Tim： He _____ (be) starving. He _____ (eat) something.

4. Billy： Cindy's phone bill is due today.

   Zoe： She _____ (pay) the bill right now, or she can't call anyone with her phone.

5. Rick： My little brother was taken to the hospital last night. He burned his fingers.

   Heather： He _____ (play) with matches any more.

10 依據對話的意思，用 may 或 should not / may not / must not 搭配括弧中的動詞完成對話。
→ Unit 65 重點複習

1. You _____ (have) one more piece of the pizza, but you _____ (eat) all of it.

2. You _____ (listen) to music on an authorized website, but you _____ (download) music from an illegal site.

3. You _____ (have) a cup of coffee a day, but you _____ (put) too much sugar in it.

4. You _____ (drive) to the bank, but you _____ (find) a parking space anywhere near the bank.

5. You _____ (call) her in the middle of the night, but she _____ (answer) the phone.

6. You _____ (watch) the lions in the zoo, but you _____ (try) to touch them.

11 依據對話的意思，用 should 或 shouldn't 搭配括弧中的動詞完成對話。

→ Unit 66 重點複習

1. Peggy：My dog Momo has been playing

　　　　 with his toy for twenty minutes.

　 James：You _____ (give)

　　　　 Momo some water to drink.

2. James：Snowbell is too fat.

　　 Anne：You _____ (feed)

　　　　　 her so much food.

3. Joanne：She looks so cute and friendly.

　　 David：I think we _____

　　　　　　(adopt) her.

4. Erica：Ted had a diarrhea this morning.

　　 Pete：You _____ (give)

　　　　　 him any more ice cream.

5. Peggy：Momo doesn't look happy today.

　 James：He just wants to play.

　　　　 You _____ (spend)

　　　　 more time with him.

6. Diana：Kiki is losing a lot of hair.

　　Jacky：That's not good. You

　　　　　 _____ (take)

　　　　　 her to a vet.

Unit **71**

Affirmative and Negative Sentences
肯定句和否定句

1 肯定句是「**描述一個肯定事實**」的句子。

I have a large family. 我有一個大家庭。

Jim went to college last year.
吉姆去年上大學。

2 否定句是「**表達否定意義**」的句子，通常句子裡會出現**否定詞 not、never**或 **rarely** 等。

I don't think it's a good idea.
我不認為這是個好主意。

I never lie to my parents.
我從不對爸媽說謊。

Nina rarely goes on a vacation. She's a workaholic.
妮娜很少去度假，她是個工作狂。

3 一般句子要構成否定句，如果是**現在式**，只要在**動詞前面加上** do not 或 does not；
如果是**過去式**，則在動詞前面加上 did not。

My grandparents don't like to live in the city. 我的祖父母不喜歡住在城市裡。

Brad doesn't believe in ghosts.
布萊德不相信世界上有鬼。

Carrie didn't take part in the competition last Wednesday.
凱莉上週三並沒有去參加比賽。

4 如果句子裡有 **be 動詞**或**情態助動詞**，則在 be 動詞或情態助動詞後面加上 not，構成否定句。

I am not mad at you. 我並不生你的氣。

Your father would not want you to stay in this industry.
你父親不會希望你待在這個行業裡。

Rene cannot scuba dive, but she loves snorkeling.
蕾妮不會水肺潛水，但是她愛浮潛。

Practice

1

將右列肯定句改寫為
否定句。

1. James is playing with his new iPhone.

   → *James isn't playing with his new iPhone.*

2. Vincent owns a shoe factory.

   → ....

3. They went to a concert last night.

   → ....

4. I enjoy reading.

   → ....

5. I can ride a unicycle.

   → ....

6. Summer vacation will begin soon.

   → ....

7. I had a nightmare last night.

   → ....

8. I am from Vietnam.

   → ....

2

將右列否定句改寫為
肯定句。

1. Sue didn't watch the football game on TV last night.

   → ....

2. Rick can't speak Japanese.

   → ....

3. Phil and Jill weren't at the office yesterday.

   → ....

4. I couldn't enter the house this morning.

   → ....

5. Joseph doesn't like spaghetti.

   → ....

6. They aren't drinking apple juice.

   → ....

7. She isn't going shopping tomorrow.

   → ....

8. I won't tell Sandy.

   → ....

Unit 72

Question Forms: Types of Questions and the Question Words "What" and "Who"

疑問句：疑問句的種類和
疑問詞 What、Who 的用法

1 疑問句是用來提出疑問的句子，必須以「問號 ?」結尾。

Are you satisfied with the results?
你對這結果滿意嗎？

Did he apologize for being rude?
他為他的無禮表示歉意了嗎？

2 一般動詞的疑問句，如果是**現在式**，必須在句首加上 Do 或 Does，後面維持**動詞原形**；如果是**過去式**，則在句首加上 Did。

Do you spend your summer on a tropical island every year?
你每年夏天都去熱帶島嶼度假嗎？

Does he jog for fifty minutes every day?
他每天慢跑五十分鐘嗎？

Did I tell you that I had passed the exam?
我有沒有告訴你我已經通過考試了？

3 be 動詞或情態助動詞的疑問句，則是將 be 動詞或情態助動詞**移至句首**。

Is there anything wrong?
有什麼不對勁嗎？

Shall we set off for the train station?
我們是不是該出發去火車站了？

Will you keep the secret? 你會保密嗎？

4 還有疑問句是在句首使用**疑問詞**。

常見的疑問詞：
① what   ⑤ who
② where   ⑥ how
③ when   ⑦ which
④ why   ⑧ whose

5 what 用來詢問「**一般事物**」，通常指**動物**或**無生物**。

Ⓐ What is your cell phone number?
Ⓑ My cell phone number is 0928-332-432.
Ⓐ 你的手機號碼是幾號？
Ⓑ 我的手機號碼是 0928-332-432。

Ⓐ What type of beverage is that?
Ⓑ It's plum green tea.
Ⓐ 那是什麼飲料？
Ⓑ 梅子綠茶。

6 who 用來詢問「**人**」。

Ⓐ Who are you?
Ⓑ I'm Jerry White.
Ⓐ 你是誰？
Ⓑ 我是傑瑞・懷特。

Ⓐ Who is your favorite author?
Ⓑ Maybe John McPhee, but that's a hard question to answer.
Ⓐ 你最喜歡的作家是誰？
Ⓑ 大概是約翰・麥克菲吧，不過這個問題很難回答。

Practice

1

將右列句子改寫為「疑問句」。

1. Jerry is good at photography.
   → *Is Jerry good at photography?*

2. Jane doesn't believe what he said.
   → _____

3. He never showed up at the party.
   → _____

4. Johnny gets up early every day.
   → _____

5. I will remember you.
   → _____

6. Julie asked me to give her a ride yesterday.
   → _____

7. She was surprised when he called.
   → _____

8. He's going to buy a gift tomorrow.
   → _____

2

依據粗體字的提示，將句子以 who 或 what 造出問句。

1. Q *What are you watching on the Internet?*
   A I'm watching **the news** on the Internet.

2. Q _____
   A I'm interested in **painting scenery**.

3. Q _____
   A **That man** is the vice president of the company.

4. Q _____
   A My favorite musician is **Bach**.

5. Q _____
   A He is looking at **a cat on the roof**.

6. Q _____
   A **Jude** is writing an email.

Unit 73

Question Forms: "Who" and "What"
Used as Subjects or Objects
疑問句：Who 和 What 作主詞或受詞的用法

1 疑問句中，who 用來指「人」，可以用來詢問句中**主詞**或**受詞**。

Susan **is calling** Leo. 蘇珊正在叫李歐。
主　詞　　　　　　　受詞

 詢問主詞
Who **is calling** Leo? 誰在叫李歐？
主　詞

 詢問受詞
Who **is** Susan **calling**? 蘇珊在叫誰？
受　詞

2 疑問句中，what 用來指「**動物或無生物**」，可以用來詢問句中**主詞**或**受詞**。

詢問主詞
What **happened**? 發生什麼事？
主　詞

詢問受詞
What **did** the dog **eat**? 這隻狗吃了什麼？
受　詞

3 who 和 what 用來詢問主詞時，**問句的動詞**和**直述句的動詞**是相同的。
詞語的順序不需要改變，也不需要另外加助動詞 do、does 或 did。

直述句	用 who 或 what 詢問主詞
Willy is eating a sandwich. 威利正在吃三明治。	Who is eating a sandwich? 誰正在吃三明治？
Debbie likes mountain climbing. 黛比喜歡爬山。	Who likes mountain climbing? 誰喜歡爬山？
Something has happened to Jim. 吉姆發生了一些事。	What has happened to Jim? 吉姆發生了什麼事？

4 who 和 what 用來**詢問受詞**時，會改變語序，或者加上 **do**、**does** 或 **did** 來構成疑問句。

直述句	用 who 或 what 詢問受詞
Willy is eating a sandwich. 威利正在吃三明治。	What is Willy eating? 威利正在吃什麼？
Debbie likes mountain climbing. 黛比喜歡爬山。	What does Debbie like? 黛比喜歡什麼？
The vase is made of plastic. 這個花瓶是塑膠做的。	What is the vase made of? 這個花瓶是什麼做的？

Practice

1

用 who 或 what 分別寫出詢問主詞和受詞的問句。

Johnny ate my slice of pizza.
→ *Who ate my slice of pizza?*
→ *What did Johnny eat?*

The boss consulted Lauren first.
→ ....
→ ....

Tom helped cook the fish.
→ ....
→ ....

My dog broke the vase.
→ ....
→ ....

Mom is making food for the baby.
→ ....
→ ....

Denise is standing next to Allen.
→ ....
→ ....

Unit 74

Question Forms: the Question Words "When," "Which," "Where," and "Whose"

疑問句：疑問詞 When、Which、Where、Whose 的用法

1 when 用來詢問「時間」。

A When **do you start to work in the morning?**
B **My job starts at 9:30 a.m.**
A 你早上幾點開始工作？
B 我的工作是從早上 9 點半開始。

A When **did you move to Taiwan?**
B **I moved to Taiwan two years ago.**
A 你是什麼時候搬到台灣的？
B 我兩年前搬到台灣。

2 which 用來詢問「選擇」。

A Which **road do I take to get to Hsinchu?**
B **To get to Hsinchu, you should take Highway 1.**
A 我要走哪一條路才能到新竹？
B 要到新竹，你必須走國道一號。

A Which **do you want, the red apple or the green apple?**
B **I want the green one.**
A 你想要哪一種，紅蘋果還是青蘋果？
B 我要青的。

3 where 用來詢問「地點」。

A Where **did you study in Germany?**
B **I studied in Berlin.**
A 你在德國的哪裡念書？
B 我在柏林念書。

A Where **do you live?**
B **I live in the Netherlands.**
A 你住在哪裡？
B 我住在荷蘭。

4 whose 用來詢問「所有權」。

A Whose **chicken is this?**
B **That chicken belongs to Colonel Sanders.**
A 這個雞肉是誰的？
B 那個雞肉是桑德斯上校的。

A Whose **books are these?**
B **These books are mine. I just bought them.**
A 這些書是誰的？
B 這些書是我的，我剛剛才買的。

5 who's 和 whose 的意思與用法皆不相同。
who's 同 who is；
而 whose 則是 who 的所有格。

Who's **going to clean up after the party?**
  ↳ = who is
派對後誰要負責清理？

Whose **cell phone is ringing?**
  ↳ whose 是 who 的所有格。
誰的手機在響？

Practice

1

下列詞彙適合做哪一個疑問詞的回答？
將它們填入正確的空格內。

	Italy	
this one	my brother's	in 2022
the blue shirt	the large one	the cat's
the taller man	last December	the mall
Amber's	the office	the garage
tomorrow	Ms. Smith's	next month

❶ which
this one

❷ where

❸ when

❹ whose

2

自下表選出正確的疑問詞填空。

where
when
whose
which

1. _____ was the Meiji Restoration in Japan?

2. _____ is Gary going to meet his client, in a café or in his office?

3. _____ city, Kyoto or Osaka, has the most beautiful temples?

4. _____ invention was the Walkman?

5. _____ is the British Museum located?

6. _____ was the steam train invented?

7. _____ bicycle is this?

8. _____ did you last see him?

9. _____ do you like better on pasta, olive oil or butter?

10. _____ does your school begin?

Unit 75

Question Forms:
the Question Words "How" and "Why"
疑問句：
疑問詞 How 和 Why 的用法

1 how 用來詢問「方法」。

Ⓐ How do you get to the zoo?

Ⓑ Take the train to the last stop, and then walk past the mall to the zoo.

Ⓐ 你是怎麼去動物園的？

Ⓑ 搭火車到最後一站，然後再經過大賣場走到動物園。

2 how 常和一些字搭配使用。

Ⓐ How tall was that dinosaur?
那隻恐龍有多高？

Ⓑ That dinosaur was 10 meters tall.
那隻恐龍有 10 公尺高。

Ⓐ How long was that dinosaur?
那隻恐龍有多長？

Ⓑ That dinosaur was 30 meters long.
那隻恐龍有 30 公尺長。

Ⓐ How much did that dinosaur weigh?
那隻恐龍有多重？

Ⓑ That dinosaur weighed over 2,500 kilograms.
那隻恐龍重達 2,500 公斤以上。

Ⓐ How many animal species have survived from the time of the dinosaurs?
有幾種動物從恐龍時代存活下來？

Ⓑ Only a few, such as sharks.
只有非常少數，像是鯊魚。

3 why 用來詢問「理由」。

Ⓐ Why did that chicken cross the road?

Ⓑ That chicken crossed the road to get to the other side.

Ⓐ 為什麼那隻雞要過馬路？

Ⓑ 過馬路是因為牠要到路的另一邊。

Ⓐ Why are you going to school?

Ⓑ I am going to school to study animal behavior.

Ⓐ 你為什麼要上學？

Ⓑ 我上學是為了研究動物行為。

How

| old 老的 | tall 高的 | long 長的 |
| much 多的 | many 多的 | often 常常 |

1

自下表選出適當的
「疑問詞彙」來完成
句子。

How
How much
How old
How long
How many
How tall
How often

1. Ⓐ _____ is your brother?

   Ⓑ He is 25 years old.

2. Ⓐ _____ is your sister?

   Ⓑ She is 160 centimeters tall.

3. Ⓐ _____ money do you have in your wallet?

   Ⓑ I have about 500 dollars in my wallet.

4. Ⓐ _____ times were you late for work this week?

   Ⓑ I was late three times this week.

5. Ⓐ _____ do I operate this machine?

   Ⓑ You can follow the instruction manual.

6. Ⓐ _____ do you see your boyfriend?

   Ⓑ I see him every weekend.

7. Ⓐ _____ is your winter break from school?

   Ⓑ My winter break is about three weeks.

8. Ⓐ _____ was your hamster when it ran away?

   Ⓑ It was over two years old.

9. Ⓐ This building is tightly guarded. _____ could he enter the manager's room?

   Ⓑ He must be a smart thief.

10. Ⓐ _____ is Taipei 101?

    Ⓑ It is about 100 stories tall.

11. Ⓐ _____ does a cup of pearl milk tea cost?

    Ⓑ It usually costs 25 dollars.

12. Ⓐ _____ do you go to Chicago to visit your relatives?

    Ⓑ I usually go to Chicago to visit my relatives twice a year.

13. Ⓐ _____ do you stay when you visit your family in Chicago?

    Ⓑ I usually stay a week or so.

14. Ⓐ _____ do I get to the airport?

    Ⓑ Use a map.

Unit 76

Question Tags
附加問句

1 附加問句是附屬於句子結尾的小問句，用來提問或確認某件事情。

Tina is single, isn't she?
蒂娜還是單身，對嗎？

Jerry doesn't have a girlfriend, does he?
傑瑞沒有女朋友，對嗎？

I can introduce them to each other, can't I?
我可以介紹他們兩個認識，不是嗎？

2 肯定句會使用**否定的**附加問句，否定句會使用**肯定的**附加問句。

We are staying here, aren't we?
我們會待在這兒，對不對？

We aren't staying here, are we?
我們不會待在這裡，對嗎？

3 **現在簡單式**的附加問句，句子裡如果**沒有 be 動詞或助動詞**（can、may、should 等），附加問句就要用 **do**、**don't**、**does** 和 **doesn't** 來構成。

You like to eat prunes, don't you?
你喜歡吃乾梅子，對不對？

Harry eats anything dead or alive, doesn't he?
不管活的還是死的東西，哈利都吃，不是嗎？

4 **過去簡單式**的附加問句，則用 **did** 和 **didn't** 來構成。

You didn't quit your job, did you?
你並沒有辭職，對嗎？

Larry stopped working at the airport, didn't he?
賴瑞不在機場工作了，不是嗎？

They got up early last weekend, didn't they?
他們上個週末很早起，不是嗎？

5 附加問句可以用來「**詢問問題**」，如果提問時**不知道答案**，語調要上揚。

This is my milk, isn't it?
這是我的牛奶，對不對？

唸唸看

He comes from Greece, doesn't he?

They aren't afraid of snakes, are they?

Ivy can't make rice pudding, can she?

6 附加問句也可用來「**確認事情**」或「**提出聲明**」。如果提問時已經知道答案，只是要做確認，語調要下降。

It's past your bedtime, isn't it?
現在已經超過你的上床時間了，對吧？

7 一般來說，**附加問句**的動詞和時態應該與前文一致，但也有例外。

She has a big house, hasn't she?
= She has a big house, doesn't she?
她有一棟大房子，對不對？

He wasn't leaving, was he?
他並沒有要離開，對吧？

例外

I am next, aren't I?
我是下一個，對不對？

1

摔角選手 Hulk（**HH**）
正在接受脫口秀主持人
DL 的訪問，請根據訪
問內容，寫出正確的「附
加問句」。

DL : Hello, Hulk. I can call you Hulk, ❶＿＿＿＿＿＿＿?

HH : I prefer Mr. Hooligan.

DL : You're joking, ❷＿＿＿＿＿＿?

HH : Of course. I don't look like a guy who stands on formality,
❸＿＿＿＿＿?

DL : You look like a guy who stands on other people's heads. I can say
that, ❹＿＿＿＿＿?

HH : Sure. I'm proud of crushing my opponents under the heels of my
boots.

DL : When you stand on your opponents, you don't hurt them,
❺＿＿＿?

HH : Hey! I haven't killed anybody yet, ❻＿＿＿＿＿?

DL : Let's go back to the beginning. You started wrestling as a child,
❼＿＿＿＿＿＿?

HH : My first real opponent was my older brother.

DL : You didn't fight with your sister, ❽＿＿＿＿＿?

HH : She was stronger than my brother, so I left her alone.

DL : You didn't wrestle with anybody else, ❾＿＿＿＿＿?

HH : We had a pet alligator.

DL : You have wrestled with alligators, ❿＿＿＿＿?

HH : Yeah, but my sister was tougher than any alligator.

DL : Who was uglier, your sister or the alligator?

HH : You don't want to make me mad, ⓫＿＿＿＿＿?

DL : No! You don't want to talk about that, ⓬＿＿＿＿?
Let's talk about your new TV show . . .

2

寫出右列句子的
附加問句。

1. You're going to adopt a stray cat, ＿＿＿＿＿?

2. He is not going abroad to study the law, ＿＿＿＿＿?

3. You can't run fast, ＿＿＿＿＿?

4. She will come to the class, ＿＿＿＿＿?

5. I passed the exam, ＿＿＿＿＿?

6. She doesn't believe me, ＿＿＿＿＿?

7. The gift is for me, ＿＿＿＿＿?

8. I'm chosen, ＿＿＿＿＿?

9. It's midnight, ＿＿＿＿＿?

10. Sam didn't cook dinner last night, ＿＿＿＿＿?

Unit 77

Imperative Sentences
祈使句

1 祈使句是用來表達「**強烈要求或命令**」的句型，肯定句以「**動詞原形**」開頭。

Stop. 住手。

Watch **your head.** 小心你的頭。

Look **both ways before crossing the street.**
過馬路之前要記得左看右看注意來車。

Walk **this way.** 走這邊。

Wait **here.** 在這裡等。

Watch **your step.** 小心你的腳步。

2 **祈使句**的否定句會使用 do not 或其縮寫 don't，也可以使用 never。

Do not **touch** the sculptures.
不要碰這些雕像。

Please do not take **pictures.**
請不要拍照。

Do not **stand** there. 不要站在那裡。

Don't **touch** the animals. 不要摸動物。

Don't **step** in the puddles. 別踩進水坑。

祈使句的使用時機

1 **Invitations** 邀請
Please **join our tour.**
一起去旅行吧。

2 **Requests** 要求
Put **your tickets here.**
把票放在這裡。

3 **Instructions** 命令
Everybody **follow me.**
所有人跟我來。

4 **Warnings** 警告
Watch **out.** 小心。

5 **Offers** 提供
Have **some green tea, please.**
喝點綠茶吧。

6 **Advice and suggestions** 建議
Take **a break.** 休息一下。

7 **Encouragement** 鼓勵
Don't **give up now.**
不要現在放棄。

8 **Pleading** 懇求
Don't **leave now.**
現在不要離開。

3 **祈使句**前後可以加上 please 表示禮貌。

Please **hurry up.** 請快一點。

Slow down, please. 請慢下來。

Please **don't pick the flowers!**
請不要摘花！

Practice

1

右列句子哪些屬於「祈使句」？請在祈使句前面打✓。

.... 1. Help yourself to that egg.

.... 2. You must talk to your teacher right away.

.... 3. Do not touch the stove.

.... 4. Can't you be honest?

.... 5. Please sit down.

.... 6. Tie your shoes this way.

.... 7. Nobody trusts Jason.

.... 8. Go back to bed now.

.... 9. I won't let you leave home.

.... 10. Don't feed your brother worms.

2

將右列句子改寫為「祈使句」。

1. Paul, I want you to close that door.

   → ....

2. You should not go out at midnight.

   → ....

3. You can't throw garbage into the toilet.

   → ....

4. Can you go buy some eggs now?

   → ....

5. I hope you're not mad at me.

   → ....

6. You can take a No. 305 bus to the city hall.

   → ....

7. You should be careful not to wake up the baby.

   → ....

8. You don't have to worry about so many things.

   → ....

9. You should relax.

   → ....

10. Why don't you do your homework right now?

    → ....

Review Test of Units 71–77
單元 71–77 總複習

1 分辨下列句子是肯定句、否定句還是疑問句。在肯定句的前面寫上 A（affirmative），在否定句的前面寫上 N（negative），在疑問句的前面寫上 Q（question）。

→ Unit 71–75 重點複習

.... 1. You can't get into that room.

.... 2. That is the best movie I've ever watched.

.... 3. Betty is never late for work.

.... 4. Am I wrong about him?

.... 5. They're not from Peru.

.... 6. Did he make these cookies by himself?

.... 7. Timmy bought two boxes of chocolate in the store.

.... 8. Have you ever seen a whale?

.... 9. What happened last night?

.... 10. I'll come back in fifteen minutes.

2 用 Who、What、Where、When、Why、How、Which 或 Whose 等疑問詞，完成填空。

→ Unit 72–75 重點複習

1. .... can I pick up my dry cleaning? Tonight or tomorrow morning?

2. .... can I get new sports shoes?

3. .... is the most famous Japanese musician?

4. .... much does a lottery ticket cost?

5. .... left the refrigerator door open?

6. .... do you want to go on a vacation? Guam?

7. .... does the plane leave for Bali?

8. .... many brothers and sisters do you have?

9. .... did you hit your sister?

10. .... should people eat a balanced diet?

11. .... train did you take on Friday night, the 9:30 p.m. train or the one at 11:30 p.m.?

12. .... is the name of the tallest mountain in the world?

13. .... of these novels did you enjoy reading the most?

14. .... are the names of the movies you have seen this month?

15. .... scooter is blocking my car?

16. .... turn is it to use the bathroom?

3 依據粗體字的提示，將句子以 who 或 what 造出問句。

→ **Unit 75 重點複習**

1. **Eve** is visiting Charles.

    → _Who is visiting Charles?_

2. Eve is visiting **Charles**.

    → ⋯⋯

3. **Edward** wants to meet Cathy.

    → ⋯⋯

4. Cathy wants to meet **Edward**.

    → ⋯⋯

5. **Mary's editing of the report** took her a long time.

    → ⋯⋯

6. He took the **birthday cake** with him.

    → ⋯⋯

7. Keith is dating **someone**.

    → ⋯⋯

8. **Something** crashed.

    → ⋯⋯

9. **Dad** answered the phone.

    → ⋯⋯

10. **Someone** wants to marry Jenny.

    → ⋯⋯

11. Dennis wants to buy **a new cell phone**.

    → ⋯⋯

12. **Dennis** wants to buy a new cell phone.

    → ⋯⋯

13. **Sylvia** wants to eat peanuts.

    → ⋯⋯

14. Sylvia wants to eat **peanuts**.

    → ⋯⋯

4 請在每一句的後面，加上正確的「附加問句」。
→ Unit 76 重點複習

1. Sightseeing is fun, _____isn't it?_____

2. Working 60 hours a week isn't good for you, _____

3. Chocolate chip cookies are tasty, _____

4. We aren't too old to have a good time, _____

5. You did a good job on the report, _____

6. You didn't get the letter in the mail, _____

7. The meeting was boring, _____

8. The project wasn't finished on time, _____

9. You liked the lentils, _____

5 請將下列錯誤的句子，更正重寫。
→ Unit 72–76 重點複習

1. Who Chris is calling?
   → _Who is Chris calling?_

2. What Irene wants to do?
   → _____

3. Who does want to stay for dinner?
   → _____

4. Who the last piece of cake finished?
   → _____

5. Who did invented the automobile?
   → _____

6. Who's dirty dishes are these on the table?
   → _____

7. What side of the road do you drive on?
   → _____

8. Rupert likes history, does he?
   → _____

9. They drive a minivan, don't it?
   → _____

6 找出下列對話中屬於「祈使句」的用法，畫上底線。
→ **Unit 77 重點複習**

Bob : How can I get to the station?

Eve : Go straight down this road. Walk for fifteen minutes and you will see a park.

Bob : So, the station is near the park.

Eve : Yes. Turn right at the park and walk for another five minutes. Cross the main road. The station will be at your left. You won't miss it.

Bob : That's very helpful of you.

Eve : Be sure not to take any small alleys on the way.

Bob : I won't. Thank you very much.

Eve : You're welcome.

7 將下列句子分別改寫為「否定句」和「疑問句」。
→ **Unit 71–75 重點複習**

1. Eddie is a naughty boy.

   → ....

   → ....

2. Jack walks to work every morning.

   → ....

   → ....

3. Sammi visited Uncle Lu last Saturday.

   → ....

   → ....

4. She will be able to finish the project next week.

   → ....

   → ....

5. My boss is going to Beijing tomorrow.

   → ....

   → ....

6. Joe has already seen the show.

   → ....

   → ....

Unit **79**

Phrasal Verbs (1)
片語動詞（1）

片語動詞（phrasal verb）和**動詞片語**（verb phrase）不同。**片語動詞**是一組固定用語，**動詞片語**則是任何一組以動詞開頭的詞組。下列兩例就是動詞片語：

- go **to work on time** 準時去上班
- watch **the game on TV** 看電視轉播的賽事

1 有時，動詞後面會加上某些**介系詞**或**副詞**，如 up 和 down，形成一組**動詞片語**，我們稱這種固定的動詞片語為**片語動詞**。

- **get along** 相處
- **find out** 發現
- **watch out** 小心

2 這些介系詞或副詞，有時會**稍微改變動詞的意義**，但我們仍能從字面上探知意義。

Throw the ball. 把球丟出去。
↳ 動詞 throw：把球投擲出去。

Throw away the ball. 把球丟掉。
↳ 片語動詞 throw away：把球扔到垃圾桶裡。

Come in from the porch.
↳ 進來室內。
從走廊上進來吧。

Come out to the porch. 出來走廊上吧。
↳ 出來室外。

3 有些**片語動詞**的意義已經與原來的動詞不相同，**產生了新的意義**。

If you are going to throw up, go into the bathroom.　↳ 吐
如果你要吐，就到廁所去。

The bank robber came out after the police cornered him.　↳ 出現
這名銀行搶匪在被警方包圍之後，只好現身。

4 片語動詞有四種類型。第一種是後面**不需要再加受詞**，可以單獨存在的片語動詞。

- **stand up** 起立
- **take off** 起飛

When you hear your name, please stand up. 叫到你的名字時請站起來。

Don't take off until I get back.
我還沒回去前先別出發。

watch out 小心
Watch out! There's a car coming.
小心！有車子來了。

shut up 閉嘴
Will you please shut up?
拜託你閉嘴好嗎？

show up 出現
Jason promised to come to the meeting, but he never showed up.
傑森答應要來開會，但一直沒出現。

go off 響起
The alarm clock went off while I was having a sweet dream.
我好夢正甜時，鬧鐘就響了。

calm down 冷靜
Calm down. I'll help you go through all this. 冷靜點，我會幫你度過這一切。

hang out 在某地逗留或與某人相處
We should hang out together at the mall sometime next week.
我們下星期找個時間在購物中心聚聚。

give up 放棄
Don't give up. 不要放棄。

Practice

1

自右表選出正確的「片語動詞」填空，並做出適當的變化，完成句子。

come along	take off	stay up	work out
move in	hang out	come in	

1. My wife didn't _____ on the trip to Egypt.

2. Curtis needs to _____ at the gym more often.

3. Why don't we _____ together next week?

4. The plane has _____. You're too late.

5. You look tired. Did you _____ late last night?

6. Another family is _____ to the neighborhood.

7. _____, please.

2

選出正確的答案。

1. Her fondest dreams have at last come **true / out**.

2. Are we going to eat **up / out** tonight?

3. I think I'll try to encourage him. He shouldn't give **up / off**.

4. Did he show **up / down** at the party? I didn't see him.

5. I'm moving **in / out** tomorrow. We'll soon become roommates.

6. Don't stand there. Sit **up / down**.

7. I'm sorry for being late. The alarm clock didn't go **on / off** this morning.

8. Fay fell **out / down** and got hurt.

9. Can I have a plastic bag? I feel like throwing **out / up**.

10. Do you get **up / on** early every day?

11. Life has to go **out / on**.

12. Where did you grow **off / up**?

Phrasal Verbs (2)
片語動詞（2）

1 第二種片語動詞必須搭配**受詞**使用，受詞的位置又有兩種，可以互換。（下面的第一種句型較為常用）

1 動詞 + 介系詞／副詞 + 受詞

• take out 拿出去　　• take off 脫掉

Can you help me take out the garbage?
可以請你幫我把垃圾拿出去丟嗎？
Take off your coat and hang it in the closet. 把外套脫下來掛到衣櫥裡。

• find out 發現

How did Jack find out everything about me? 傑克是怎麼知道我的每一件事情的？

2 動詞 + 受詞 + 介系詞／副詞

• bring in 拿進來　　• bring up 養育

Bring the laundry in before it rains.
趁下雨之前把衣服收進來。
We are trying to bring our son up to be considerate and responsible.
我們盡力把我們的兒子培養得既體貼又有責任感。

假如受詞是代名詞，就只能放在**動詞和介系詞或副詞的中間**。

• bring up 告訴；提起　　• carry out 進行

• I will bring it up with Craig.
　　↳ it = project
我會對克雷格提起這項計畫。

look up 查閱
Pan looked up the word in the dictionary.
→ Pan looked the word up in the dictionary.
潘在字典裡查了這個字。

fill out 填寫
Please fill out the form.
→ Please fill it out.
請填妥這張表格。

call off 取消
They called off the game because of rain.
→ They called it off because of rain.
他們因雨取消了這場比賽。

turn up/down 調大聲／調小聲
Turn down the volume.
→ Turn it down.
把聲音調小一點。

turn on/off 打開／關閉
He turned on the light and started to read.
→ He turned the light on and started to read.
他開燈開始看書。

hand in 繳交
You have to hand in the paper on Monday.
→ You have to hand the paper in on Monday.
請在星期一繳交報告。

put out 撲滅
The firefighter put out the fire within an hour.
→ The firefighter put the fire out within an hour.
消防人員在一小時內撲滅了火勢。

set off 點燃
They set off the fireworks.
→ They set the fireworks off.
他們點燃爆竹。

turn down 拒絕
The manager turned down his proposal.
→ The manager turned his proposal down.
經理推翻了他的提議。

1

自下表選出正確的
「片語動詞」來填空，
並依照範例，用另
外兩種句型來改寫句
子。

set off

turn down

try on

call off

take off

fill out

throw away

bring up

turn off

1. Dick and Byron _____ *set off* _____ the fire crackers.

   → *Dick and Byron set the fire crackers off.*

   → *Dick and Byron set them off.*

2. Don't _____ the price tag in case we have to return the sweater.

   → _____

   → _____

3. Don't _____ the offer right away.

   → _____

   → _____

4. We don't _____ bottles if they can be recycled.

   → _____

   → _____

5. You need to _____ the form and attach two photos.

   → _____

   → _____

6. Would you like to _____ these shoes?

   → _____

   → _____

7. Could you _____ the radio? I don't want to listen to it.

   → _____

   → _____

8. I'll have to _____ the meeting.

   → _____

   → _____

9. Lucy _____ her son by herself.

   → _____

   → _____

Unit **81**

Phrasal Verbs (3)
片語動詞（3）

1 第三種也必須搭配**受詞**使用，而且受詞只能**放在整個片語動詞的後面**。

3 | 動詞 | + | 介系詞／副詞 | + | **受詞** |

- take after 相似
- pull for 支持

Your daughter takes after your wife.
你女兒很像你太太。

The crowd is pulling for the home team.
群眾全力支持地主隊。

apply for 申請
I have already applied for the job.
我已經去應徵這份工作了。

arrive in 抵達
Gina arrived in Athens on Saturday.
吉娜於星期六抵達了雅典。

depend on 依靠
Success depends on hard work.
成功端賴努力。

look after 照顧
Could you look after the baby on weekends?
週末都可以麻煩你照顧寶寶嗎？

look for 尋找
Scientists are looking for some rare elements.
科學家們在尋找一些稀有元素。

belong to 屬於
This suitcase belongs to Mr. Jefferson.
這個公事包是傑佛遜先生的。

run into 遇見
I ran into an old friend on my way home.
我在回家的路上遇到一位老朋友。

2 第四種由「**動詞 + 副詞 + 介系詞**」組成較長的片語動詞，並且必須在最後面加上**受詞**。

4 | 動詞 | + | 副詞 | + | 介系詞 | + | **受詞** |

- look forward to 期待
- move away from 搬離

Walter is looking forward to a break after finishing the IPO.
在完成公司初次公開上市的工作之後，華特很期待能小休一下。

Nicole is moving away from home for the first time.
這是妮可第一次離開家。

keep away from 遠離
Keep away from the broken windows.
遠離碎裂的窗戶。

keep up with 跟上
I can't keep up with you when we are jogging.
慢跑的時候我一直跟不上你。

catch up with 趕上
You should study hard to catch up with your classmates.
你要用功才能趕上你同學。

get along with 與……相處
I can't get along with Susan.
我跟蘇珊無法相處。

put up with 忍受
I can't put up with him any more.
我再也受不了他了。

fed up with 受夠
Shut up. I'm fed up with your lies.
不要再說了，我聽夠了你的謊言。

Practice

1

自下表選出正確的「片語動詞」填空，完成句子。

| catch up with |
| come across |
| run down |
| watch out for |
| get over |
| put up with |
| fed up with |
| look after |

1. It's hard to _____ other people's kids.

2. _____ the bucket on the floor.

3. You can leave now, and I will _____ you later.

4. I can _____ almost anything except screaming babies.

5. If you _____ any wooden napkin rings, please let me know.

6. Donna is _____ the street noise at her apartment and is planning to move.

7. The editor asked me to _____ the facts on this story.

8. She'll _____ her disappointment and face the reality.

2

自下表選出適當的「介系詞」填空，完成句子。

| up |
| down |
| on |
| in |
| of |
| into |
| out of |
| to |
| from |
| off |
| for |

1. I got _____ the train at Angel Street and got _____ at the main station.

2. It's starting to rain. Let's get _____ the car before it pours.

3. I ran _____ Jack this morning. He was in a hurry, so we didn't talk.

4. Thank you for coming. I look forward _____ seeing you next time.

5. After I got _____ the taxi, I went into the fish store.

6. We ran out _____ toilet paper. I'll buy some this afternoon.

7. Winnie applied _____ the scholarship last week.

8. I know I can rely _____ him.

9. Does this locker belong _____ Sean?

10. Norman arrived _____ New York yesterday.

11. What are you looking _____?

1 自右表選出適當的片語動詞，填空完成句子。
→ Unit 79–81 重點複習

1. Please _____ me _____ at seven tomorrow morning. I don't want to sleep late.
2. Alison is going to _____ with her friends at the Internet café tonight.
3. The plane is going to _____ soon. We have to _____ the plane right away.
4. When are we going to _____ this report?
5. Sam _____ his old cell phone and bought a new one.
6. When are you going to _____ to your new apartment?
7. _____ the car now.
8. _____ the grass. Don't step on it.
9. Please _____ the registration form.
10. We are _____ each other very well.
11. She walks so fast. I can hardly _____ her.
12. Could you _____ Janet on your way to the office?
13. I _____ in the country, but I'm living in the city now.
14. Aunt Sally _____ her two kids all by herself.
15. Pete: Where is Tony?
    Ron: He is _____ at the gym.
16. The vice president is not available tomorrow. We'll have to _____ the meeting.
17. He finished the conversation with Zoe and _____ the phone.
18. May I _____ this coat?

get in

throw away

take off

hang out

wake up

pick up

work out

call off

get on

hand in

grow up

fill out

get along with

bring up

move in

keep away from

hang up

keep up with

try on

2 自下表選出適當的「副詞」或「介系詞」，搭配題目上方標示的動詞構成片語動詞，填空完成句子。
→ Unit 79–81 重點複習

| up | down | in | out | on | off | after | away | for |

look

1. I'm .... my wallet. Did you see it?

2. .... the meaning of this phrasal verb in your electronic dictionary.

3. I have to .... my little brother on Saturday.

4. ....! Don't trip over that wire.

turn

5. Could you .... the heat, please? It's too hot.

6. Why not .... the TV and relax?

7. Don't .... this offer, because it's the best you are going to get.

8. Make sure you .... the lights before going to bed.

take

9. Could you .... the garbage now?

10. .... your sunglasses so that I can see your eyes.

11. The plane will .... in a few minutes.

12. I don't .... my father. I look like my mother.

put

13. It's cold outside. You should .... a coat.

14. We .... the campfire and left the park.

15. Don't .... the plan until tomorrow.

16. He .... his toys and went to bed.

go

17. I'm back. Please .... with the story.

18. The fire alarm .... at midnight.

19. They .... for a date.

Unit 83

Adjectives
形容詞

不論描述的名詞是單數、複數,男性、女性,或者前面加什麼冠詞,形容詞的型態都**不需改變**。

- a new phone
- the new phone
- two new phones
- a tall boy
- the tall boy
- two tall boys

1 形容詞是「**描述人物、地方、物品或狀況**」的詞彙,用來**修飾名詞**。

an old computer
一台老舊的電腦

the smart dog
這隻聰明的狗

a fast car
一輛很快的車

2 形容詞經常放在**名詞**的前面。

1 形容詞 + 名詞

Watch out for the sharp edge.
小心那鋒利的邊。

He's an old professor. 他是位老教授。

That's a powerful squirt gun.
那是把強力水槍。

That's a warm coat.
那是件溫暖的大衣。

It's a deep river.
這是條很深的河。

3 形容詞也可放在 **be 動詞**或**連綴動詞**的後面。

2 主詞 + be 動詞／連綴動詞 + 形容詞

The news was sad. 這則消息很感傷。

The car looks cool. 這輛車看起來很酷。

My aunt feels lonely. 我嬸嬸覺得很寂寞。

The soup seems spicy.
這碗湯好像很辣。

The office is messy.
這間辦公室很髒亂。

- He's a ¹_____ guy. 他是個好人。
- Those ²_____ people are laughing.
那群開心的人在開懷大笑。

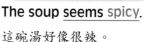

- Her husband ³_____.
她的先生個子很高。
- The fish ⁴_____.
這魚聞起來很香。

Practice

1

自下表選出適當的「形容詞」，搭配圖片的名詞完成填空。

big
small
old
new
soft
hard
curved
straight

1 pants

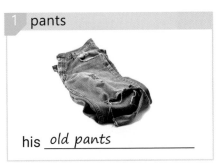

his _old pants_____

2 pants

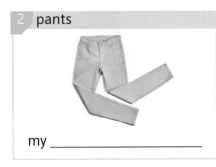

my _____

3 chair

a _____

4 chair

a _____

5 dog

her _____

6 dog

her _____

7 road

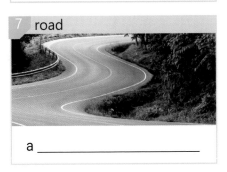

a _____

8 road

a _____

2

將右列各組詞彙重組，以正確語序完成句子。

1. he in lives town small a

   → ....

2. eyes blue she has

   → ....

3. smells the lamb stew good

   → ....

4. two I have kids lovely

   → ....

5. cute is my teddy bear

   → ....

Unit **84**

Adverbs and Adverbial Phrases
副詞和副詞片語

1 副詞是用來修飾**動詞**、**形容詞**或是**另一個副詞**的詞彙。由好幾個詞彙所組成的副詞,則稱為**副詞片語**。

I work in the Bangkok office one week each month.
↳ one week each month 是副詞片語。
我每個月都有一星期到曼谷分公司上班。

I never rest when I'm on the road. It's always hard work.
↳ never 和 always 都是副詞。
我不曾在途中休息,這一直都是很辛苦的工作。

2 副詞經常由形容詞轉變而來。

1 形容詞直接加上 **ly**。
① cold → cold**ly** 冷地
② beautiful → beautiful**ly** 美麗地
③ rapid → rapid**ly** 迅速地

2 字尾是「子音 + **y**」的形容詞,去掉 **y** 再加 **ily**。
① handy → hand**ily** 便利地
② ready → read**ily** 敏捷地
③ easy → eas**ily** 輕易地

3 字尾是「子音 + **le**」的形容詞,去掉 **le** 再加 **ly**。
① horrible → horrib**ly** 恐怖地
② possible → possib**ly** 可能地
③ simple → simp**ly** 純粹地

形容詞 It was an easy job.
這是個輕鬆的工作。

副詞 We finished the job easily.
我們很輕鬆地完成工作。

3 有些副詞的構成較**不規則**。

1 副詞和形容詞完全不一樣。
good → well 好地

2 副詞和形容詞一樣。
early → early 早地
fast → fast 快速地

3 一個形容詞演變出兩種副詞形式,且意義相同。
clean → clean/cleanly 俐落地
bright → bright/brightly 明亮地

形容詞 It was a clean getaway.
這是一次徹底的逃脫。

副詞 He got away cleanly.
他逃得無影無蹤。

副詞 He has clean forgotten it.
他完全忘記這件事了。

4 副詞的位置通常在**動詞後面**,或者在**受詞的後面**。

Henry clapped wildly. 亨利熱烈地鼓掌。

Paula welcomed me warmly.
寶拉熱情地歡迎我。

The agent signed the contract sadly.
代理商傷心地簽下合約。

1

寫出右列形容詞所對應的副詞。

1. sudden _____
2. real _____
3. early _____
4. quick _____
5. good _____
6. final _____
7. fast _____
8. lazy _____
9. entire _____
10. gentle _____
11. lucky _____
12. cheap _____
13. probable _____
14. special _____
15. cheerful _____
16. deep _____
17. merry _____
18. clean _____
19. simple _____
20. angry _____

2

運用粗體字的「副詞」形式，搭配括弧內提示的動詞，改寫各個句子。

1. He gave a **clear** answer. (answer)
   → *He answered clearly.*

2. He's a **bad** singer. (sing)
   → _____

3. He was **late** for school. (arrive)
   → _____

4. She's a **good** painter. (paint)
   → _____

5. She's a **fast** learner. (learn)
   → _____

6. He's a **noisy** worker. (work)
   → _____

7. She's a **professional** translator. (translate)
   → _____

8. It was a **terrible** earthquake. (tremble)
   → _____

9. She's a **fast** reader. (read)
   → _____

10. She's a **frequent** shopper. (shop)
    → _____

Unit 85

Adverbs and Adverbial Phrases of Time and Place
時間副詞和地方副詞

1 時間副詞或副詞片語是用來指出「**事情發生的時間**」。
一般放在**動詞後面**，若句中有受詞，則要放在受詞**後面**。

- later 晚一點
- early 早
- tomorrow 明天
- this morning 今天早上
- on Thanksgiving 在感恩節
- at midnight 在半夜

1

主詞	+	動詞	+	時間副詞	
The plane		arrived		late.	這班飛機誤點了。
Ladies		go		first.	女士優先。

2

主詞	+	動詞	+	受詞	+	時間副詞	
He		brushes		his teeth		in the morning.	他早上刷牙。
She		baked		the cake		before the party.	她在派對開始前烤了一個蛋糕。

2 地方副詞或副詞片語是用來指出「**事情發生的地點**」。
和時間副詞一樣，地方副詞一般放在**動詞後面**，若句中有受詞，則要放在受詞**後面**。

- here 這裡
- there 那裡
- down 下面
- outdoors 戶外
- at the park 在公園
- to the club 往俱樂部

3

主詞	+	動詞	+	地方副詞	
He		lives		in the suburbs.	他住在郊外。
The newspaper		was		in the mailbox.	報紙在信箱裡。

4

主詞	+	動詞	+	受詞	+	地方副詞	
Wally		parked		the car		in the driveway.	華利把車子停在車道上。
Erica		took		the box		to the post office.	艾麗卡把箱子拿去郵局。

時間副詞和**地方副詞**通常不會放在動詞和受詞的中間。

✗ We ate at the restaurant dinner.
✓ We ate dinner at the restaurant.
✗ We eat at 7 p.m. dinner.
✓ We eat dinner at 7 p.m.

3 如果句中有時間副詞也有地方副詞，通常時間副詞會放在地方副詞的**後面**。

5

主詞	+	動詞（片語）	+	地方副詞	+	時間副詞
Ronald		ate his lunch		behind the store		after the delivery truck left.

貨車離開後，雷諾在商店後吃午餐。

| Judy | | walked | | to Suzy's house | | on Saturday afternoon. |

茱蒂在星期六下午走路到蘇西家。

| Trent | | had a party | | in his house | | on Christmas day. |

聖誕節那天，崔特在他家舉辦派對。

Practice

1

將右列各組詞彙重組，
以正確的語序完成句子。

1. over there   my parents   live
   → *My parents live over there.*

2. they bought   over 20 years ago   the house
   → ....

3. pays the mortgage   on the first day of each month
   my dad   to the bank
   → ....

   ....

4. went   he   to check the mailbox   downstairs
   → ....

5. to Wendy's house   were delivered   this morning   no packages
   → ....

6. Jack and Jimmy   at the café   are going to meet   this afternoon
   → ....

2

依提示回答問題。

1. When and where did you leave the bag?
   (in the cloakroom / at 4:30 yesterday)
   → ....

2. When and where did you last see him?
   (on January 22nd / at Teresa's birthday party)
   → ....

3. When and where did you buy that book?
   (last week / at the bookstore around the corner)
   → ....

4. When and where do you go swimming?
   (at the health club / on Sundays)
   → ....

5. When and where did you learn to dive?
   (three years ago / at the Pacific Diving Club)
   → ....

6. When and where did you eat lunch yesterday?
   (at Susie's Pizza House / at 12:30)
   → ....

Adverbs and Adverbial Phrases of Frequency and Manner
頻率副詞和狀態副詞

1 頻率副詞是用來指出「**事情多常發生**」的副詞，通常放在**主要動詞的前面**。

- **always** 總是
- **rarely** 很少
- **sometimes** 有時
- **often** 時常
- **usually** 經常
- **never** 不曾

1 　主詞　+　頻率副詞　+　動詞

Morty always **eats** lunch at his desk.
莫提總是在他的辦公桌吃午餐。

I rarely **drink** coffee at night.
我晚上很少喝咖啡。

We often **develop** plans as a team.
我們通常團隊一起構思企畫。

David never **remembers** his dreams.
大衛從來不記得他做過的夢。

2 頻率副詞也可以放在 be 動詞的後面。

2 　主詞　+　be 動詞　+　頻率副詞

Frank is sometimes **sent** to pick up a customer at the airport.
法蘭克有時會被派去機場接客戶。

Cab lines are usually long at the airport.
機場的計程車隊通常會排很長。

I am always glad they send Frank to the airport, because I hate driving on the highway.
他們派法蘭克去機場我都會很高興，因為我很討厭在高速公路上開車。

3 如果是頻率副詞片語，通常會放在句尾。

- **every evening** 每天晚上
- **once a week** 每週一次
- **four times** 四次
- **every day** 每天

I buy a new teddy bear once a year.
我每年都會買一個新的泰迪熊。

I sleep with my teddy bear every night.
我每天晚上都和我的泰迪熊一起睡。

I watch the news on TV every evening.
我每晚都收看電視新聞。

4 狀態副詞是用來描述「**事情發生時的狀態**」，一般放在**動詞或受詞的後面**。

She is typing.
她正在打字。

She is typing fast.
她正在迅速地打字。

She reads carefully.
她很仔細地閱讀。

The car stopped suddenly.
這輛車突然停下來。

Practice

1

將右列各組詞彙重組，以正確的語序完成句子。

1. he   misses   never   the mortgage payment

   → ....

2. is   in the morning   always   the first customer   he

   → ....

3. he   to work   walks   every day

   → ....

4. the water   quickly   overflowed

   → ....

5. exploded   suddenly   the volcano

   → ....

6. many burglaries   lately   have been   there

   → ....

7. entirely   their minds   that   changed

   → ....

2

依據事實，使用「頻率副詞」回答右列問題。

1. How often do you go to school?

   → ....

2. How often do you exercise?

   → ....

3. How often do you go on a trip to a foreign country?

   → ....

4. How often do you go to a movie?

   → ....

5. How often do you do the dishes?

   → ....

6. How often do you visit your grandparents?

   → ....

7. How often do you eat fast food?

   → ....

8. How often do you work on Saturdays?

   → ....

Comparison of Adjectives
形容詞的比較級與最高級

原級		比較級		最高級	
young	年輕的	younger	較年輕的	youngest	最年輕的
big	大的	bigger	較大的	biggest	最大的
beautiful	美的	more beautiful	較美的	most beautiful	最美的
		less beautiful	較不美的	least beautiful	最不美的

1 形容詞有三種形態：**原級**、**比較級**和**最高級**，用來表示**修飾**的程度。

原級 Look at that old ship. 看那艘老舊的船。

比較級 That ship is as old as my great grandfather.
那艘船就跟我的曾祖父一樣老。

比較級 If there is an older one, I don't see it.
我還沒看過比這更舊的船。

最高級 That is the oldest ship at the dock.
那是碼頭裡最舊的一艘船。

2 比較級用來比較**兩個事物**；最高級用來比較**三個以上的事物**。

Your kite is higher than my kite, but his kite is the highest.
你的風箏飛得比我的高，但是他的風箏飛得最高。

3 形容詞比較級和最高級的構成方式：

1 單音節的形容詞，其比較級和最高級，是在字尾分別加 er 和 est。

原級	比較級	最高級
tight 緊的	tighter	tightest
small 小的	smaller	smallest

2 單音節的形容詞，若字尾是「短母音＋子音」，其比較級和最高級必須先重覆字尾，再加 er 和 est。

原級	比較級	最高級
big 大的	bigger	biggest
hot 熱的	hotter	hottest

3 單音節的形容詞，若字尾是 e，其比較級和最高級，應直接加 r 和 st。

原級	比較級	最高級
cute 可愛的	cuter	cutest
late 遲的	later	latest

4 雙音節的形容詞，若字尾是「子音＋y」，其比較級和最高級必須先去掉 y，再加上 ier 和 iest。

原級	比較級	最高級
sloppy 懶散的	sloppier	sloppiest
foggy 有霧的	foggier	foggiest

5 雙音節形容詞，若字尾非 y，其比較級和最高級，是在形容詞前加上 more/less 和 most/least。more 和 most 具正面意義，而 less 和 least 則具反面意義。

原級	比較級	最高級
special 特別的	more special	most special
famous 有名的	less famous	least famous

6 三個音節以上的形容詞，其比較級和最高級，也同樣是在形容詞前加 more/less 和 most/least。

原級	比較級	最高級
aggressive 進取的	more aggressive	most aggressive
colorless 黯淡的	less colorless	least colorless

7 有些形容詞的比較級和最高級屬於**不規則變化**，請逐一牢記。

原級	比較級	最高級
good 好的	better	best
bad 壞的	worse	worst

Practice

1

寫出右列形容詞的比較級和最高級。

1. big _____
2. tall _____
3. close _____
4. fast _____
5. sad _____
6. cute _____
7. spicy _____
8. thin _____
9. good _____
10. many _____

11. large _____
12. late _____
13. busy _____
14. simple _____
15. tiny _____
16. bad _____
17. useful _____
18. little _____
19. quiet _____
20. high _____

2

將括弧內的形容詞以「最高級」的形式填空，來詢問「誰是最……的人」。並依據事實回答問題。

1. Who is _____ (cute) in your class?

→ _____

2. Who is _____ (hardworking) in your class?

→ _____

3. Who is _____ (funny) in your class?

→ _____

4. Who is _____ (boring) in your class?

→ _____

5. Who is _____ (friendly) in your class?

→ _____

6. Who is _____ (tall) in your class?

→ _____

7. Who is _____ (smart) in your class?

→ _____

8. Who is _____ (creative) in your class?

→ _____

Unit 88

Patterns Used for Comparison
表示「比較」的句型

1 我們可以用形容詞的**比較級**來比較兩件事物，後面需搭配 than 來使用。

1 A + is/are + 形容詞比較級 + than + B

The Nile River is longer than the Yellow River. 尼羅河比黃河長。

My running shoes are cooler than your running shoes. 我的慢跑鞋比你的酷。

Your hair is more colorful than my hair.
你的頭髮顏色比我的鮮豔。

2 我們可以用形容詞的**最高級**來比較三樣或三樣以上的事物，前面需加 the。

2 A + is/are + the + 形容詞最高級

That is the tallest building in the city. ↳ 這城市有三座以上的高樓。
那是這座城市最高的大樓。

She is the most amazing
↳ 我見過三個以上令人驚嘆的女子。
woman I have ever met.
她是我見過最不可思議的女子。

This is the worst restaurant I've ever eaten at. ↳ 我吃過三家以上不好吃的餐廳。
這是我吃過最難吃的餐廳。

3 若要形容兩個人、事、物是一樣的，可用 as . . . as。

3 A + is/are + as + 形容詞原級 + as + B

Your cubicle is as ugly as mine.
你的隔間跟我的一樣醜。

Your hands are as cold as mine.
你的手跟我的一樣冰。

4 若要形容兩個人、事、物是不一樣的，可用 not as . . . as。

4 A + is/are + not + as + 形容詞原級 + as + B

My boss isn't as bad as your boss. 我老闆不像你老闆那麼壞。

I'm not as slow as you.
我才沒你那麼慢。

5 上述用法中，than 和 as 後面通常會接**受詞代名詞**。

Even my grandmother is stronger than you. 就連我祖母都比你還強壯。

He sold as many computers as me.
他賣的電腦和我一樣多。

6 如果在很正式的用法裡，than 和 as 後面會接「**主詞代名詞 + 動詞**」。

My brother is smarter than I am.
我弟比我聰明。

I'm not as smart as he is.
我沒有他那麼聰明。

But I'm bigger than he is.
但是我個子比他大。

依據圖示，用下表的詞彙，以 A is . . . than B 的句型來描述 Jim 和 Ken 的不同。

1

short	professional	fat
tall	casual	business-like
intense	lighthearted	

1. *Ken is shorter than Jim.*
2. _____
3. _____
4. _____
5. _____
6. _____
7. _____
8. _____

Jim

Ken

2

將錯誤的句子打×，
並寫出正確的句子。
若句子無誤，則在方
框內打 ✓。

1. Mt. Everest is highest mountain in the world.

   ☒ *Mt. Everest is the highest mountain in the world.*

2. The Japan Trench is deeper the Java Trench, but the Mariana Trench is deepest.

   ☐ _____
   _____

3. Africa is not as large than Asia.

   ☐ _____

4. Blue whales are the larger animal in the world.

   ☐ _____

5. A giant rabbit can grow as big as a labrador.　★ labrador：拉布拉多，一種獵犬。

   ☐ _____

6. China is not as more democratic as the United States.

   ☐ _____

7. The Burj Dubai is tallest than Taipei 101.

   ☐ _____

8. The Pacific Ocean is larger than the Indian Ocean.

   ☐ _____

Unit **89**

"Too" and "Enough" With Adjectives and Adverbs
Too 和 Enough 搭配形容詞或副詞的用法

1 too 用來指出某人或某物「太……」，要放在**形容詞或副詞的前面**。

1 | too | + | 形容詞 |

I can't see. It's <u>too foggy</u>.
我看不見，霧太濃了。

2 | too | + | 副詞 |

Hurry up. You're walking <u>too slow</u>.
快一點，你走得太慢了。

2 enough 的意思是「**足夠的**」，必須在形容詞或副詞的後面。

3 | 形容詞 | + | enough |

You can't wear my clothes. You aren't <u>big enough</u>.
你不能穿我的衣服，你的體型不夠大。

4 | 副詞 | + | enough |

I can't read your phone number. You're not writing <u>clearly enough</u>.
我看不到你的電話號碼，你寫得不夠清楚。

3 too 和 enough 後面，可接「for + 受詞」。

5 | too | + | 形容詞／副詞 | + | for | + | 受詞 |

I found a studio apartment, but it was <u>too expensive for you</u>. 我找到一間公寓套房，但對你而言太貴了。

6 | 形容詞／副詞 | + | enough | + | for | + | 受詞 |

The apartment is <u>cheap enough for me</u>.
這間公寓對我而言夠便宜了。

4 too 和 enough 後面，也常接「加 to 的不定詞」。

7 | too | + | 形容詞／副詞 | + | 受詞 |

This bar is <u>too noisy to hold</u> a conversation.
酒吧太吵了，無法談話。

8 | 形容詞／副詞 | + | enough | + | to V |

This café is <u>quiet enough to read</u>.
這家咖啡廳夠安靜，可以讀書。

5 too 和 enough 後面如果有受詞也有動作，就可以用「for . . . to V」的句型。

9 | too | + | 形容詞 | + | for | + | 受詞 | + | to V |

It was <u>too noisy for me to read</u>.
太吵了，我無法看書。

10 | 形容詞／副詞 | + | enough | + | for | + | 受詞 | + | to V |

It wasn't <u>quiet enough for him to read</u>.
不夠安靜，他無法看書。

6 too 和 very 有時稱為**程度副詞**；too 表「**過量**」或「**超過需要**」；而 very 則是用來**修飾**或**強調**形容詞。

Terry is a fast swimmer.
She swims <u>very fast</u>.

↳ very 用來強調她游得多快。

泰瑞是位游泳健將，她游得非常快。

Larry is not a good swimmer, and he has been underwater <u>too long</u>.

↳ too 表示他已超過他應該待在水底的時間。

賴瑞不太會游泳，他已經待在水底太久了。

Practice

1

這些工作場合有什麼問題？請依據圖示，自下表選出適當的形容詞或副詞，用「too ...」的句型造句，描述圖片中狀況。

1. Charlie couldn't talk on the phone because it was _____.

2. Amy couldn't take a coffee break because there were _____ phone calls.

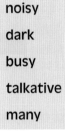

noisy
dark
busy
talkative
many

3. Andrew couldn't see the keyboard very well because it was _____.

4. Jessica couldn't help her colleagues with their work because she was _____.

5. Jennifer couldn't concentrate on her work because her colleagues were _____.

2

使用右表的句型，改寫上一大題的句子。

too ... (for sb.) to ...

1. *It was too noisy for Charlie to talk on the phone.*
2. _____
3. _____
   _____
4. _____
   _____
5. _____
   _____

Unit 90

Review Test of Units 83–89
單元 83–89 總複習

1 依據圖示，自下表選出適當的詞彙，用 is 或 look 來造句。
→ Unit 83 重點複習

| fat | healthy | tall | short |
| strong | weak | happy | thoughtful |

1. He is/looks strong.
2. _____
3. _____
4. _____
5. _____
6. _____
7. _____
8. _____

2 選出正確的答案。
→ Unit 83-84 重點複習

1. It was a **clear / clearly** day.

2. He loved her **dear / dearly**.

3. It was a **fair / fairly** shot.

4. The decision was **just / justly**.

5. It was a **wide / widely** river.

6. The bunny ran **quick / quickly**.

7. He was **wrong / wrongly** accused.

8. The balloon drifted **slow / slowly**.

9. She drove home **careful / carefully**.

3 將下列詞彙依正確的語序重組，並在結尾加上句號或問號，完成句子。
→ **Unit 83–86** 重點複習

1. guy   handsome   a   is   He
   → *He is a handsome guy.*

2. handsome   is   guy   That
   → _____

3. to his office   takes the subway   Ned
   → _____

4. to take a break   ready   Penny   is   always
   → _____

5. terrible   is   driver   a   Dennis
   → _____

6. Dennis   terribly   drives
   → _____

7. I'm   to   excited   too   wait
   → _____

8. these gifts   for   big   enough   isn't   This bag
   → _____

9. Do you   here   work   in this building
   → _____

10. Does Larry   with his brother   fight   every day
    → _____

11. Did we   at the Italian restaurant   meet   last Monday night
    → _____

12. Does Mr. Harrison   eat lunch   always   at the same time
    → _____

13. Is Greg   late   usually   for his tennis date
    → _____

14. Does Frederica   to the spa   go   every week
    → _____

15. Are you   too tired   to get up   sometimes   in the morning
    → _____

4 依據圖示，自字彙表選出適當的頻率副詞填空。

→ **Unit 86** 重點複習

1. Meg reads newspapers ....

2. Tom drives to work ....

3. Luke .... drinks coffee.

4. Jason .... eats French fries.

5. Steve .... takes vitamins.

never
often
twice a week
every day
sometimes

---

5 依據圖示，自字彙表選出適當的頻率副詞填空，完成句子。

→ **Unit 86** 重點複習

every week   every weekend
always   every Sunday
six times a month

1. Jason goes to church
....

2. Lily goes to the gym
....

3. Kate .... goes
   swimming on Tuesday.

4. Timmy doesn't wash his
   laundry ....

5. I go out with my friends
   ....

6 將下列錯誤的句子打✗，並寫出正確的句子。若句子無誤，則在方框內打 ✓。
→ Unit 88 重點複習

1. I see two talls guys.

   ☒ *I see two tall guys.*

2. That is a tall guy.

   ☐ ....

3. Tony is tallest than David.

   ☐ ....

4. Who is the most tall guy in the room?

   ☐ ....

5. John is taller than Sam.

   ☐ ....

6. James is gooder at math than Robert.

   ☐ ....

7. Irving is a happily guy.

   ☐ ....

8. Janice speaks English very good.

   ☐ ....

7 依據圖示，自下表選出適當的「副詞」填空，完成句子。
→ Unit 88 重點複習

| quietly |
| slowly |
| joyfully |
| eagerly |

1 ▶

Kitty is sleeping .... on the grass.

2 ▶

The sisters are pillow fighting ....

3 ▶

Dori is chewing the bone ....

4 ▶

My turtle swims ....

8 用「not as . . . as」的句型，來比較圖中這些地方。

→ **Unit 88** 重點複習

Canada
Greenland Iceland Germany
Sweden
Switzerland
Area: 836,109 sq mi
Area: 674,843 km²
Area: 41,285 km²
Russia
Area: 6,592,800 sq mi
Mt. Everest
Height: 8,848 m

Per Capita Income: 30,644 US dollars
Seoul

France
Spain
Italy
Mexico

Mt. Fuji
Height: 3,776 m

Tokyo
Population: 37,393,000

Egypt

Brazil
Area: 3,287,597 sq mi

Madagascar
Area: 226,597 sq mi

Manila
Population: 13,923,452

Per Capita Income: 4,135 US dollars
Jakarta

1. Mt. Fuji and Mt. Everest (tall)

   → ....

2. Brazil and Russia (big)

   → ....

3. Madagascar and Greenland (big)

   → ....

4. Jakarta and Seoul (prosperous)

   → ....

5. Manila and Tokyo (densely populated)

   → ....

6. France and Switzerland (small)

   → ....

7. Iceland and Spain (far south)

   → ....

8. Italy and Germany (far north)

   → ....

9. Canada and Mexico (hot)

   → ....

10. Egypt and Sweden (cold)

   → ....

9 自字彙表選出適當的形容詞，用題目指定的句型寫出「表示比較」的句子。
→ Unit 88–89 重點複習

. . . than

1. An orange is _____ a lemon.

2. A coat is _____ a shirt.

3. Florida is _____ than Michigan.

the . . .

4. The Antarctica is _____ place on earth.

5. The Jupiter is _____ planet in our solar system.

6. Taipei 101 is _____ building in Taiwan.

as . . . as

7. Earthquakes are _____ typhoons.

8. Can a horse run _____ a train?

9. Can a kite fly _____ an eagle?

big
high
terrible
tall
fast
hot
warm
sweet
cold

10 依據題意，將括弧裡的單字搭配 too 或 enough 填空。有些題目可有兩種寫法。
→ Unit 89 重點複習

1. You have worked _____. (hard)

2. Don't work _____. (late)

3. This soup is _____. (salty)

4. This curry isn't _____. (spicy)

5. The way you speak is _____. (blunt)

6. Your music is _____. (loud)

7. This cell phone is _____. (expensive)

8. This computer is _____. (slow)

Unit **91**

Prepositions of Place: in, on, at (1)
表示地點的介系詞：in、on、at（1）

in the box
在箱子裡

on the box
在箱子上

at the bottom
of the pole
在燈柱底部

 1　in 可用來指出「在某個三度空間裡」。

There's a fly in my soup.
我的湯裡面有隻蒼蠅。

I keep my emergency money in the refrigerator.
我把緊急備用的錢放在冰箱裡。

Barbara is in line to buy train tickets.
芭芭拉在排隊買車票。

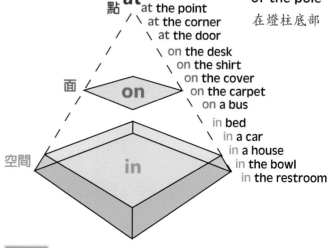

點 **at** at the point
　　　　　　at the corner
　　　　　　at the door
　　　　　　　on the desk
　　　　　　　on the shirt
面 **on** 　　on the cover
　　　　　　on the carpet
　　　　　　　on a bus
　　　　　　　in bed
　　　　　　　in a car
空間 **in** 　in a house
　　　　　　in the bowl
　　　　　　in the restroom

2　on 可用來表示「在表面上」。

Put the money on the counter.
把錢放在櫃台上。

Write your name and phone number on this paper.
把你的名字和電話號碼寫在這張紙上。

Put the stamp on this envelope.
把郵票貼在這個信封上。

4　at 可用來表示「在某一點上」。

Meet me at the corner of 43rd Street and Lexington.
到列克星頓和第 43 街的轉角跟我碰面。

You can buy cheesecloth at the farmers' market.
你可以在農產品集貨市場買到薄紗布。

比較

- Your tablet is in my schoolbag.
  你的平板在我的書包裡。
- My schoolbag is on the table by the door.
  我的書包擺在門邊的桌上。
- I paused the bluetooth speaker at the beginning of the fourth song.
  我把藍芽音響暫停在第四首歌一開始的地方。

3　on 也可用來表示「在一條線上」或「在某物的邊緣」。

There is a tag on the cable.
電纜線上有個標籤。

Hang the laundry on the clothesline.
把洗好的衣服掛在曬衣繩上。

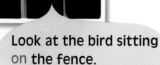
Look at the bird sitting on the fence.
你看棲息在籬笆上的那隻鳥。

Practice

1

根據圖示，用 in、on 或 at 填空，完成句子。

This dog is ＿＿＿＿ the sofa.

This dog is ＿＿＿＿ the dog house.

Jack is ＿＿＿＿ the end of the line.

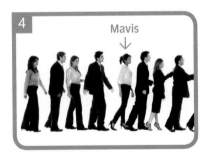

Mavis is ＿＿＿＿ the middle of the line.

This cat is ＿＿＿＿ the cup.

I'd like some whipped cream ＿＿＿＿ my coffee.

There's a magazine ＿＿＿＿ the table.

Ben is jumping ＿＿＿＿ the bed.

The geese are standing ＿＿＿＿ the edge of a river.

Part 12 Prepositions 介系詞

Unit 92

Prepositions of Place: in, on, at (2)
表示地點的介系詞：in、on、at（2）

in Australia
在澳洲

in Sydney
在雪梨

at home 在家

---

1 in 常與**城鎮、洲名、縣市、國家、大陸**名稱連用。

Sydney is in Australia. 雪梨在澳洲。

I live in Sydney. 我住在雪梨。

2 at 常與「**具體的小地點**」連用。
at home、at work 是慣用語。

Otto is at the library, but he will be back for dinner.
奧圖現在在圖書館，但是他會回來吃晚餐。

I'll be at home if you need me.
如果你需要我，我會在家裡。

He is at home in the suburbs.
他在位於郊區的家中。

I'll be at work this afternoon from 1:00 to 5:00. 今天下午 1 點到 5 點，我要上班。

He is at work now if you want to call him there.
他現在在上班，你可以打電話去那裡。

3 at 也可表示「**在學習或研究的地方**」。

She is a kindergarten teacher at Tiny Tots Language School.
她是 Tiny Tots 語言學校的幼稚園老師。

I saw Tom at school yesterday.
我昨天在學校看見湯姆。

4 at 和 in 可用來談論「**在某個建築物裡面**」。

He met her at the multiplex movie theater.　　↳ inside or outside
他和她在電影城見面。

The mayor's office is in the City Hall.
市長的辦公室在市政廳裡。　　↳ inside

5 談論「**建築物本身**」時，要用 in 這個字。

There is an elevator in the Eiffel Tower.
艾菲爾鐵塔裡有電梯。

There are spas in the rooms in the Hot Spring Hotel.
溫泉旅館的房間裡有溫泉水療。

6 來看看 in 、at 和 on 在「**地址**」裡的用法。

國家／洲名 → in

I live in California. 我住在加州。
I live in the U.S.A. 我住在美國。

城市／鄉鎮 → in

I live in Mendocino. 我住在孟得昔諾。

街道 → on

I live on Flores Street. 我住在福羅爾斯街。

門牌號碼 → at

I live at 323 Flores Street.
我住在福羅爾斯街 323 號。

樓層 → on

I live on the fifth floor. 我住在五樓。

Practice

1

用 in 或 at 填空，完成句子。

1 There are many people .... the airport.

2 The kids are .... school.

3 There are some people .... the train station.

4 Vicky is .... the library.

2

依據圖示，用 in、on 或 at 填空，完成句子。

To: Sherman Johnson
Apt. 3F, 223 Oak Street
Evansville, Indiana, 56082, U.S.A.

1. Sherman Johnson lives .... the U.S.A.
2. He lives .... the third floor.
3. He lives .... Oak Street.
4. He lives .... 223 Oak Street.
5. He lives .... Evansville.
6. He lives .... Indiana.

Unit **93**

Other Prepositions Of Place
其他表示地點的介系詞

❶ in 在……之內

in **the box** 在箱子裡

❷ on 在……之上

有接觸到

on **the box** 在箱子上

❸ over 在……之上

正上方
沒接觸到

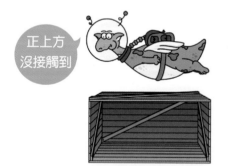

over **the box** 在箱子上方

❹ under 在……之下

正下方

under **the box** 在箱子下方

❺ in front of 在……前面

in front of **the box**
在箱子前面

❻ behind 在……後面

behind **the box**
在箱子後面

❼ near 在……附近／**next to** 緊鄰著……

near / next to **the box**
在箱子附近／在箱子旁

❽ between 在……之間

between **the box** 在箱子之間

❾ across
穿越……

❿ against
倚靠著……

across **the line**
穿越繩索

against **the box**
倚靠箱子

Practice

1 根據圖示，自下表選出適當的介系詞填空，完成句子。可重複選取。

in	on	near	next to	in front of
behind	between	over	under	against

1. The frog is _____ the leaf.

2. The woman is standing _____ the bicycle.

3. The boy is sleeping _____ the car.

4. The man is sitting _____ the bicycle.

5. The woman is resting _____ a tree and _____ a bike.

6. The girl is sleeping _____ the teddy bear.

7. The taxi stopped _____ the hotel.

8. The car is driving _____ the highway.

9. The man is hiding _____ the desk.

10. The seagull is flying _____ the ocean.

11. The dog is _____ the boys.

12. The white-headed cat is leaning _____ the black-headed cat.

Unit 94

Prepositions Of Movement
表示移動方向的介系詞

❶ into
到……之內

into the
telephone booth
到電話亭內

❷ out of
到……之外

out of the
telephone booth
到電話亭外

❸ onto 到……之上

onto the box
到箱子之上

❹ off 離開……

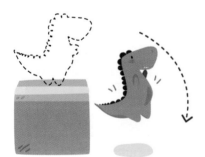

Off the box
離開箱子

❺ up
往……上

❻ down
往……下

up the hill
往山丘上

down the hill
往山丘下

❼ to 往……

❽ from 從……

from the city
從城市

to the city 往城市

❾ across 橫越／跨越

across the road
橫越馬路

❿ along 沿著／順著

along the road
沿著馬路

⓫ past 經過

past a traffic light
經過紅綠燈

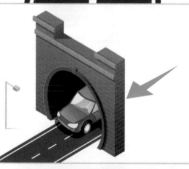

⓬ through
穿越／通過

through
the tunnel
穿越隧道

⓭ around
圍繞

around the
traffic circle
圍繞圓環

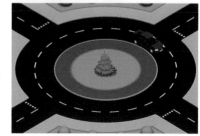

Practice

1 根據圖示，自下表選出適當的介系詞填空，完成句子。可重複選取。

into	out of	on	off	up	around
through	across	along	past	down	

The kids are partially .... the car.

The man is throwing garbage .... the trash can.

The man is walking .... the hill.

Someone is pouring water .... the instant noodles.

You need to drive .... the traffic circle.

The dolphin is jumping .... the water.

These taxis are driving .... the road.

The pedestrians are walking .... the street.

Are we going to drive .... the tunnel?

The kayaker in the yellow boat went .... the other kayaker.

Gordon is looking .... at Marty.

The woman fell .... the bike.

Prepositions of Time: in, on, at (1)
表示時間的介系詞：in、on、at（1）

1 「一天中特定的時間」，也就是「幾點幾分」，要用 at。

I have to turn in this report at 3:00.
我必須在 3 點交出這份報告。
At 5:00 I leave the office no matter what is happening.
不管發生什麼事，我都會在 5 點下班。

2 「一天中的某個時段」要用 in。

Breakfast restaurants are only open in the morning. 早餐店只有早上營業。
I like to drink coffee and read the book in the afternoon.
我喜歡在下午喝咖啡看書。

↗at night

但「在晚上」卻用 at night。
• He always gets lost at night. 他晚上老是迷路。

3 「星期」要用 on。

We are going to meet at the night market on Friday. 我們星期五約在夜市見面。
On Saturdays I always sleep late.
星期六我通常睡到很晚。

4 「星期幾的某個時段」也要用 on。

I like to watch movies on Friday nights after the kids go to bed.
我喜歡在星期五晚上孩子們都上床後看電影。
Let's go to the farmers' market on Saturday morning.
我們星期六上午到農產品市集去吧。

5 「週末」常用 on。

Are you going to the Music Festival on the weekend?
↳ 英式用 at the weekend。
你週末要去參加音樂慶典嗎？
On weekends I catch up with all my housework.
我都在週末把所有的家事做完。

6 「假日期間」會用 at；「假期當天」卻用 on。

We visit her every year at Thanksgiving.
我們每年感恩節都會去看她。
I always gain weight at Christmas.
我一到聖誕節就會變胖。
I love to eat turkey and stuffing on Thanksgiving Day.
我很喜歡在感恩節那天吃火雞肉和火雞裡的填料。
We stay up to see in the new year on New Year's Eve.
我們會在除夕夜徹夜不眠迎接新年。

Practice

1

將列表這些表示「時間的詞彙」，依據其應該搭配的介系詞，填入正確的空格內。

❶ _____ in _____

❷ _____ on _____

the morning
Friday afternoons
National Day
the weekend
Sundays
Christmas
night
Monday
6 o'clock
the evening
Christmas Day

❸ _____ at _____

2

用 in、on 或 at 填空，完成句子。

1. Meet me _____ 5:00.

2. Let's go to a baseball game _____ Saturday.

3. The store isn't open _____ the morning.

4. I only play online games _____ night.

5. I do my laundry _____ Sunday afternoons.

6. The best time to go there is _____ Independence Day.

7. I need to get up _____ 6:20 tomorrow morning.

8. We usually go to the traditional market _____ weekends.

9. I'm going to give my mom a dress as a gift _____ Mother's Day.

10. What are you going to do _____ your birthday?

Unit 96

Prepositions of Time: in, on, at (2)
表示時間的介系詞：in、on、at（2）

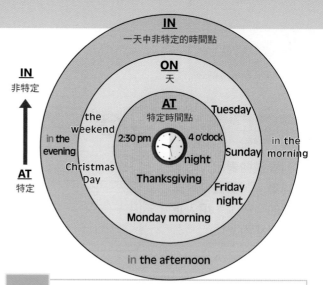

IN
一天中非特定的時間點

ON
天

AT
特定時間點

IN
非特定

AT
特定

the weekend
in the evening
Christmas Day
2:30 pm
night
Thanksgiving
Monday morning
4 o'clock
Tuesday
Sunday
Friday night
in the morning
in the afternoon

---

1 月分要用 in。

I suggest we take our vacation in August this year. 我建議我們今年八月去渡假。

My uncle wants to visit us in January.
我叔叔想要在一月時來拜訪我們。

2 日期要用 on。

February

M	T	W	T	F	S	S
				1	2	3
4	5	6	7	8	9	10
11	12	13	(14)	15	16	17
18	19	20	21	22	23	24
25	26	27	28	29		

Valentine's Day is on February 14.
情人節是在 2 月 14 日。

Spring break starts on April 1.
春假從 4 月 1 日開始。

My wife's birthday is on July 10.
我太太的生日是 7 月 10 日。

比較

• Let's go in September.
我們九月去吧。

• I am free on September 26th.
我 9 月 26 日那天有空。

• Are you free on that day?
你那天有空嗎？

3 年分要用 in。

He graduated from college in 1995.
他 1995 年從大學畢業。

The company was founded in 1888.
這間公司創立於 1888 年。

4 季節要用 in。

in the spring
in the summer
in the fall
in the winter

Flowers bloom in the spring.
花朵在春天綻放。

Mosquitoes bite most in the summer and fall. 蚊子在夏天和秋天的時候最為猖獗。

5 若已經用 this、next、every、tomorrow 或 yesterday 等表示「某特定時間」，便不可以再加 in、on 或 at。

Are you free this afternoon?
你今天下午有空嗎？

Do you want to go next week?
你下星期想要去嗎？

Let's go to the spa every Friday.
我們每星期五去做溫泉水療吧。

Can you spare an hour to help me tomorrow?
你明天可以抽出一小時來幫我嗎？

What happened to you yesterday?
你昨天發生了什麼事？

Practice

1

將列表這些表示「時間的詞彙」，依據其應該搭配的介系詞，或者是不需要介系詞，填入正確的空格內。

1 _____ in _____

2 _____ on _____

3 _____ ✗ _____

this weekend
winter
tomorrow afternoon
May 5
next summer
yesterday morning
October
1998
last month
the fall
June 27

2

用 in 或 on 填空，完成句子。
若不需要介系詞，請畫上「✗」。

1. He was born _____ 1971.
2. She was born _____ December 22, 1975.
3. The school basketball season is _____ the winter.
4. Edward is leaving this country _____ July 1st.
5. This book will be in print _____ April.
6. Jenny does her laundry _____ every Saturday.
7. We need to hand in this report _____ next Tuesday.
8. The museum is free _____ Sunday.
9. The room rates in this hotel are cheaper _____ December, January, and February.
10. Our hotel is always full _____ the summer.

Prepositions of Time or Duration: For, Since (Compared With "ago")
表示時間的介系詞：For、Since（與 ago 比較）

1 ago 是副詞，指「在……之前」，只能用於**過去式**，不能用**現在完成式**。

Steve left ten minutes ago.
↳ 從現在算起的 10 分鐘前
史帝夫 10 分鐘前離開了。

He graduated from Central University ten years ago.
↳ 從現在算起的 10 年前
他 10 年前從中央大學畢業。

I climbed the mountain three months ago.
我三個月前去爬過山。

I saw him five minutes ago.
我五分鐘前見過他。

2 時間單位要放在 ago 的「前面」。

two days ago 兩天前

two months ago 兩個月前

two years ago 兩年前

I played the song five minutes ago.
我五分鐘前播放這首歌。

3 for 用來表「時間的長短」，後面會接「一段時間」。

We have been working for hours.
我們已經工作好幾個小時了。

We stayed in Venice for five days.
我們在威尼斯待了五天。

I haven't seen him for three years.
我已經三年沒見到他了。

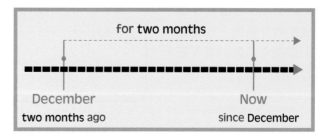

for two months

December
two months ago

Now
since December

4 since 表示「從當時到現在的時間」，用來討論過去到現在的這段時間裡所發生的事。

It has been two years since I last saw him.
從我上次見到他到現在已經兩年了。

We have been corresponding by email since then.
從那次之後，我們一直都用電子郵件通信。

I haven't talked to him since 2017.
從 2017 年之後，我就沒和他說過話了。

5 since 後面接「事情開始的時間」。

• since 11:00 從 11 點起
• since Monday 從星期一起
• since January 從一月起
• since 2018 從 2018 年
• since my brother was born 從我弟出生以來

6 for 和 since 都可用於**完成式**，表達「從過去進行到現在的時間長短」。

He has been waiting since 10:00.
他從 10 點等到現在。

He has waited for one hour.
他已經等了一個鐘頭了。

Practice

1

依據事實，用 ago
回答問題。

1. When did you move to your current apartment?

   →_____

2. When did you buy your cell phone?

   →_____

3. When did you have your last vacation?

   →_____

4. When did you meet your best friend?

   →_____

5. When did you have your last math exam?

   →_____

2

右列表示時間的詞
彙，應該搭配 for 還
是 since 使用？

請在空格內填入正確
的介系詞。

1. _____ Thursday
2. _____ last week
3. _____ one year
4. _____ 30 minutes
5. _____ 8 o'clock
6. _____ 2019

7. _____ last year
8. _____ two months
9. _____ a day or two
10. _____ we last met
11. _____ a while
12. _____ the beginning

3

依據事實，分別用
for 或 since 的兩種
句型回答問題。

1. How long have you been learning English?

   →_____

   →_____

2. How long have you lived in your current apartment?

   →_____

   →_____

3. How long have you had your own computer?

   →_____

   →_____

4. How long have you been styling your hair this way?

   →_____

   →_____

1 寫出下列詞彙的反義詞。
→ Unit 93-94 重點複習

1. in front of ⟷ ....
2. to ⟷ ....
3. over ⟷ ....

4. up ⟷ ....
5. onto ⟷ ....
6. into ⟷ ....

2 依據圖示，自下表選出適當的表示地點或位置的介系詞來填空，完成句子。
→ Unit 91-94 重點複習

in	on	past	against	over	under	to
along	into	out of	down	behind	near	between

The strawberries are .... the box.

The blueberry tarts are .... the plate.

I put some peanut butter .... the toast.

The apple is .... the books.

I poured some coffee .... the cup.

She is taking a jar of pickles .... the refrigerator.

He is putting some chicken .... his mouth.

The piece of ice is floating .... the sea.

The cheese is

....

the two halves of the bun.

Sheep B is standing

.... Sheep A.

The bees are flying

.... the flowers.

These camels are

walking .... the

desert.

The crab is moving

.... the beach.

This turtle is

swimming ....

a group of fish.

The dog has a tennis

ball .... his

mouth.

She is sitting ....

her suitcase.

The lions are ....

a car.

She is staying

.... the surface

of the water.

The man is walking

.... his room.

She is walking

.... the stairs.

3 請用 at、in 或 on 填空，完成句子。
→ Unit 91–95 重點複習

1. The box is ＿＿＿＿ the table by the door.

2. His office is ＿＿＿＿ your bus route.

3. He is expecting you ＿＿＿＿ 9 a.m.

4. He says he will be ＿＿＿＿ work all day.

5. Are you going to be ＿＿＿＿ school all day today?

6. Can you run another errand for me ＿＿＿＿ the train station?

7. I need you to get some tickets ＿＿＿＿ the lobby of the station.

8. Take the tickets to Tony's house ＿＿＿＿ Glendale.

9. She is living ＿＿＿＿ 109 Spring Street.

10. She is ＿＿＿＿ the first floor.

11. She is ＿＿＿＿ Apartment 110.

4 請用 in、on 或 at 填空，完成句子。
→ Unit 95-96 重點複習

1. My family always gets together ＿＿＿＿ Thanksgiving Day.

2. My class starts ＿＿＿＿ 8:10.

3. What are you going to do ＿＿＿＿ Tuesday?

4. I'm going jogging with my wife ＿＿＿＿ the morning.

5. He usually watches sports games on TV ＿＿＿＿ night.

6. Aunt Betty goes to church ＿＿＿＿ Sunday mornings.

7. Uncle Bob goes fishing ＿＿＿＿ the weekend.

8. We get together with our grandparents ＿＿＿＿ Christmas. We always have a feast ＿＿＿＿ Christmas Day.

9. Mr. and Mrs. Smith are going on a vacation ＿＿＿＿ July. They will leave for Australia ＿＿＿＿ July 5.

10. The restaurant was founded ＿＿＿＿ 1977.

11. Jeff always goes surfing ＿＿＿＿ the summer.

5 依據圖示，自下表選出正確的介系詞填空，完成句子。

→ **Unit 93** 重點複習

| between | behind | near | opposite | next to |
| in front of | in | on | under | |

1. The ball is .... his foot. His foot is .... the ball.

2. The ball is .... the net.

3. Player A is .... Player B.

4. Player B is .... Player A.

5. Players A and B are .... Players C and D.

6. Player E is .... to Player F.

7. Player G is running .... Player H.

8. Player K is .... Players J and L.

6 以下內容是關於一名男子和他擁有車子的經歷，請用 ago、for 或 since 填空，完成句子。
→ Unit 97 重點複習

1. I drove my first car _____ four years.

2. I crashed it while I was a college student, and I couldn't afford to buy another car _____ a long time.

3. My father told me to save my money and buy a used car. I have owned several used cars _____ then.

4. I bought my first used car 16 years _____.

5. It was a piece of junk, and I only drove it _____ two months before it broke down.

6. I drove my second used car _____ three months, and then the transmission broke.

7. I bought my third "good" used car about 15 years _____ . I loved that car very much.

8. It lasted _____ five years, and then the cost of repairs forced me to get rid of it. I decided to buy another "good" used car.

9. I have gone through five more used cars _____ I got rid of my third used car. I'm still driving a used car, and I will probably continue to do so until I can't drive any more.

7 根據題目的內容，用 **ago** 重新造句。
→ Unit 97 重點複習

1. It's 4:00 now. Dana left the office at 3:00.
   → *Dana left an hour ago.*

2. It's 4:35 now. Nancy walked out of the office at 4:00.
   → ....

3. It's 9:00 now. Victor called at 6:00.
   → ....

4. Today is Friday. Julie came on Monday morning.
   → ....

5. This is July. It happened last month on the same date.
   → ....

6. It's 2022. We saw her last year.
   → ....

8 選出正確的答案。
→ Unit 97 重點複習

1. It's 6:00. The 5:00 bus left an hour **ago / since**.

2. My sister **left / has left** to go home two days ago.

3. We walked along the beach **for / since** three hours.

4. I have been visiting my grandparents **for / since** a week.

5. She has been visiting her grandparents **for / since** Saturday.

6. I have had this car **since / for** I was 21 years old.

And, But, Or, Because, So
連接詞 And、But、Or、Because、So

1 連接詞用來**連接兩個詞彙、兩個片語**或**兩個句子的詞**。

- and
- but
- or
- so
- because
- when
- if
- before
- after

I'll take a hamburger and French fries.
我要一個漢堡和薯條。
I love fries, but I hate ketchup.
我喜歡薯條，可是我討厭番茄醬。
Sometimes I have a cola or a lemon drink.
有時我會喝可樂或檸檬飲料。
I eat fast food because it tastes good.
我吃速食是因為它好吃。
I know it's not healthy, so I don't eat it often. 我知道它不健康，所以我不常吃。

2 and、but 和 or 可用來**連接句中個別的部分**。
and 是用來連接「同類型」的字。

My grandmother has two cats and two dogs. 我奶奶有兩隻貓和兩隻狗。
We have salty and sweet bread.
我們有鹹的和甜的麵包。

3 but 用來表達「相反的概念」。

I went to his office, but he wasn't there.
我到他的辦公室去，可是他不在。
I tried to call him, but his voice mail kept picking up the call.
我打電話給他，但一直轉到語音信箱。

4 or 用來表達「多者擇一」的可能性。

We could go on a vacation to Hong Kong or Macau. 我們可以到香港或澳門度假。
Are you married or single?
你已婚還是單身？

5 because 用來描述「原因」，常連接子句。表示原因的子句會放在 because 後面。

I can't go because my wife won't let me.
我不能去，因為我太太不讓我去。
I can go because my wife is out of town.
我可以去，因為我太太出城去了。

6 so 用來描述「結果或目的」，也是連接子句。表示結果或目的的子句會放在 so 的後面。

The meeting is cancelled, so you don't have to go now.
會議取消，所以你現在不用去了。
They want to meet you right now, so you have to come as soon as you can.
他們想馬上見你，所以你得儘快趕來。

1

請用 and、but 或 or
連接右列句子。

1. I like soda. I like potato chips.

   → ....

   ....

2. Do you want to leave at night? Do you want to leave in the morning?

   → ....

   ....

3. I can't cook. I can barbecue.

   → ....

   ....

4. I have been to Switzerland. I have been to New Zealand.

   → ....

   ....

5. She isn't a ballet dancer. She is a great hip hop dancer.

   → ....

   ....

6. Tom says he is rich. He always borrows money from me.

   → ....

   ....

7. Will you come this week? Will you come next week?

   → ....

   ....

8. Shall we sit in the front? Shall we sit in the back?

   → ....

   ....

9. I read comic books. I read novels.

   → ....

   ....

10. Do you like to eat German food? Do you like to eat French food?

    → ....

    ....

When, If, Before, After
連接詞 When、If、Before、After

1 when 和 if 都連接子句。when 常用來表達「**將來確定會發生的事**」。

I'll drive you in the morning <u>when you go</u> to senior high school.
等你上高中的時候，我早上會載你去上學。

You can talk to him <u>when he gets here</u>.
當他到這裡時，你可以跟他談談。

I'll be your best man <u>when you get</u> married.
你結婚時，我會當你的伴郎。

2 if 用來表達「**不確定是否會發生的事情**」。

We'll talk about buying you a scooter <u>if your grades improve</u>.
如果你成績進步，我們再談買機車給你的事。

We'll find the money <u>if you get into UCLA</u>.
假如你申請上加州大學洛杉磯分校，我們就出錢供你念。

I'll throw you a big party <u>if you get that job</u>.
如果你得到那份工作，我就幫你辦一場盛大的派對。

3 when 和 if 的後面，都要用**簡單現在式**來表示**未來**，不可以用 will 的句型。

I will call you <u>when I am free</u>.
我有空的時候會打給你。

I will come <u>if you invite me</u>.
如果你邀請我，我就會來。

4 when 和 if 放在句首時，句中需**加逗號**。

<u>When you need a ride</u>, give me a call.
當你需要人來載你時，打個電話給我。

<u>If you come back to Taipei</u>, give me a call.
如果你回來台北，打電話給我。

5 before 和 after 也常連接子句。before 用來表示「**在某事或某時之前發生的事**」。

before   after

I have to finish this project <u>before the manager comes back</u>.
我要在經理回來之前完成這件案子。

Everybody left the party <u>before Jacky arrived</u>.
傑克還沒到，大家就已經走光了。

6 after 用來表示「**在某事或某時之後發生的事**」。

I'll meet you at the basketball court <u>after I finish cleaning my room</u>.
等我整理完房間，我就去籃球場找你。

He set out for Paris right <u>after he came back from Tokyo</u>.
他從東京回來，旋即又前往巴黎。

Practice

1

依據圖示，分別自兩個右表選出適當的片語，用「if . . . , . . . will . . .」的句型造句。

lift weights	learn lots of things
read widely	become self-confident
practice writing	increase her stamina
practice public speaking	build up his muscles
skip dessert	stay slim
often go jogging	improve his communication skills

If he lifts weights, he will build up his muscles.

....

....

....

....

....

....

....

....

....

....

....

....

....

2 利用題目給的片語，用「when she . . . , she'll . . .」的句型造句。

1. start jogging   finish stretching

   → ....

2. rest on a bench   get tired

   → ....

3 get home   eat breakfast

   → ....

1 以「I missed our date . . .」做句首，用 because 或 so 完成句子。
→ Unit 99 重點複習

1. my car broke down

   → I missed our date _____ .

2. my boss needed me to work late in the office

   → I missed our date _____ .

3. I could finish my report

   → I missed our date _____ .

4. I had to bake cookies

   → I missed our date _____ .

5. my dog was sick

   → I missed our date _____ .

6. I could see my favorite TV show

   → I missed our date _____ .

7. I had to take a sick friend to the hospital

   → I missed our date _____ .

8. I had to help my mom clean the house

   → I missed our date _____ .

2 請用 and、but 或 or 填空，完成句子。
→ Unit 99 重點複習

1. I love to eat pepperoni pizza _____ watch TV.

2. I like action movies, _____ my husband likes romantic comedies.

3. Are you going to see a doctor _____ not?

4. My mother _____ father want to come over this weekend.

5. You can quit school, _____ it's not a good idea.

6. Do you want to stay single _____ get married?

7. He has a double major in law _____ accounting.

8. I haven't graduated yet, _____ I will soon.

9. You can come with our group _____ go with the other group.

10. He will join the Army _____ go to graduate school.

3 請用 when 或 if 填空，完成句子。
→ Unit 100 重點複習

1. I want to be in the delivery room in the hospital _____ the baby is born.

2. I will buy pink baby clothes _____ it is a girl.

3. My brother will drive us home _____ we leave the hospital.

4. I will take care of the baby _____ it cries between feedings at night.

5. The baby will have a nice new crib _____ it comes home from the hospital.

6. I can't wait to find out _____ it is a boy or a girl.

7. _____ the baby is two years old, I want to have a second child.

8. _____ the first child is a boy, then I want a second boy.

9. Two boys can play together _____ they are young.

10. _____ we have a boy and a girl, I am worried they won't play together.

4 請依據提示，在第一格填入 when 或 if，並在第二格用簡單現在式或 will 的句型完成句子。
→ Unit 100 重點複習

1. _____ I get dressed tomorrow morning, I _____ (wear) my holiest jeans.

2. Perhaps Linda will be at the party. _____ I see her, I _____ (ask) her out on a date.

3. I'm definitely going to do it next time I see her. I'll give her my business card _____ I _____ (ask) her out.

4. I hope she says yes. _____ she agrees, I _____ (take) her to the aquarium to see the new killer whales.

5. Maybe that's too weird. She will probably think I am strange _____ I _____ (tell) her we are going the aquarium.

6. I know what I will do. _____ I ask her out, I _____ (give) her the choice of where to go.

5 請用 before 或 after 填空，完成句子。
→ Unit 100 重點複習

1. Spring comes _____ winter and _____ summer.

2. The lightning came _____ the thunder.

3. It began to rain _____ the thunder.

4. It rained heavily _____ the sky turned bright.

5. Sometimes there will be a rainbow _____ the rain.

Unit **102**

Numbers: Cardinal Numbers
數字：基數

1 數字分三種形式：**基數**、**序數**和**分數**。基數是用來表達**明確的數量或範圍**。序數是表**先後順序**。分數是表**非整體或少於 1 的數目**。

- **one** 一
- **two** 二
- **three** 三

- **first** 第一
- **second** 第二
- **third** 第三

- **one-third** 三分之一
- **two-thirds** 三分之二
- **one-fourth** 四分之一

2 基數從 0 到 29 的寫法：

zero	0	ten	10	twenty	20
one	1	eleven	11	twenty-one	21
two	2	twelve	12	twenty-two	22
three	3	thirteen	13	twenty-three	23
four	4	fourteen	14	twenty-four	24
five	5	fifteen	15	twenty-five	25
six	6	sixteen	16	twenty-six	26
seven	7	seventeen	17	twenty-seven	27
eight	8	eighteen	18	twenty-eight	28
nine	9	nineteen	19	twenty-nine	29

21 到 99 之間的複合數字，中間都要加連字號。
- **twenty-one**
- **ninety-nine**

3 基數從 10 到 90，以十位數為單位的寫法：

ten	10	sixty	60
twenty	20	seventy	70
thirty	30	eighty	80
forty	40	ninety	90
fifty	50		

4 數目 100 以上的數字，十位數和個位數之間，需加 **and** 來表示。

one hundred	100
one hundred and one	101
one hundred and ten	110
one hundred and twenty	120
one hundred and twenty-one	121
one hundred and ninety-nine	199
two hundred	200

5 數字 1000 以上的寫法：

one thousand	1,000	一千
ten thousand	10,000	一萬
one hundred thousand	100,000	十萬
one million	1,000,000	一百萬
one billion	1,000,000,000	十億
one trillion	1,000,000,000,000	一兆

6 hundred（百）、thousand（千）、million（百萬）或 billion（十億）的後面，都**不可加 s** 表示複數。

- **three hundred** 三百
- **three thousand** 三千
- **three million** 三百萬
- **three billion** 三十億

電話號碼的唸法，通常是一個數字、一個數字地唸。

電話號碼	5236-8813 five two three six eight eight one three
台灣地區電話號碼 （含國碼與區碼）	886-2-7612-0096 eight eight six, dash, two, dash, seven six one two, dash, zero zero nine six
含通行密碼、國碼、區碼和分機號碼	001-1-202-347-1000 Ext.2022 zero zero one, dash, one, dash, two zero two, dash, three four seven, dash, one zero zero zero, extension two zero two two

1

請用英文寫出右列
數字的唸法。

1. 9 _____

2. 13 _____

3. 78 _____

4. 141 _____

5. 385 _____

6. 7,064 _____

_____

7. 9,856 _____

_____

8. 10,231 _____

9. 1,032,540 _____

10. 6,837,650 _____

_____

11. 40,000,000 _____

12. 12,452,689 _____

_____

2

請用英文寫出右列
電話號碼的唸法。

1. 911
→ _____

2. 8786-5239
→ _____

3. 318-926-5273
→ _____

4. 003-1-250-764-5320
→ _____

_____

5. 02-3276-9370
→ _____

6. 0932-540-696
→ _____

7. 2364-5839 Ext.12
→ _____

_____

Unit 103

Numbers: Ordinal N2umbers
數字：序數

40	40th	fortieth
50	50th	fiftieth
60	60th	sixtieth
70	70th	seventieth
80	80th	eightieth
90	90th	ninetieth
100	100th	one hundredth
200	200th	two hundredth
1,000	1,000th	one thousandth
1,000,000	1,000,000th	one millionth

1 序數用來表達**先後順序**。大多數的序數是在數字後面加上 **th**，但 1、2、3 的序數是例外。「零」則沒有序數。

1	1st	first		11	11th	eleventh		21	21st	twenty-first
2	2nd	second		12	12th	twelfth		22	22nd	twenty-second
3	3rd	third		13	13th	thirteenth		23	23rd	twenty-third
4	4th	fourth		14	14th	fourteenth		24	24th	twenty-fourth
5	5th	fifth		15	15th	fifteenth		25	25th	twenty-fifth
6	6th	sixth		16	16th	sixteenth		26	26th	twenty-sixth
7	7th	seventh		17	17th	seventeenth		27	27th	twenty-seventh
8	8th	eighth		18	18th	eighteenth		28	28th	twenty-eighth
9	9th	ninth		19	19th	nineteenth		29	29th	twenty-ninth
10	10th	tenth		20	20th	twentieth		30	30th	thirtieth

2 序數前通常需要加 **the**。

He was the **first** prize winner.
他是第一特獎的贏家。

The door to his office is the **third** one on the left.
他的辦公室在左邊第三個門。

4 序數經常用來描述**日期**。

Are you free on the fifteenth of November?
你 11 月 15 日有沒有空？

Our flight departs on the second of May.
我們的班機 5 月 2 日起飛。

3 序數經常用來描述**樓層**。

I bought the lipstick on the second **floor** of the department store.
我在百貨公司的二樓買了這條口紅。

I live on the fifth **floor** of this apartment building.
我住在這棟公寓的五樓。

1

根據右列的美國歷任總統表，依範例
用序數來描述各任美國總統。

1. George Washington was _____
   President of the United States.

2. Thomas Jefferson was _____
   President of the United States.

3. James Madison was _____
   President of the United States.

4. Abraham Lincoln was _____
   President of the United States.

5. Warren Harding was _____
   President of the United States.

6. Franklin Roosevelt was _____
   President of the United States.

7. John Kennedy was _____
   President of the United States.

8. Richard Nixon was _____
   President of the United States.

9. Bill Clinton served as _____
   President of the United States.

10. Barack Obama is _____
    President of the United States.

1	1789–1797	George Washington
2	1797–1801	John Adams
3	1801–1809	Thomas Jefferson
4	1809–1817	James Madison
5	1817–1825	James Monroe
6	1825–1829	John Quincy Adams
7	1829–1837	Andrew Jackson
8	1837–1841	Martin Van Buren
9	1841	William Harrison
10	1841–1845	John Tyler
11	1845–1849	James Polk
12	1849–1850	Zachary Taylor
13	1850–1853	Millard Fillmore
14	1853–1857	Franklin Pierce
15	1857–1861	James Buchanan
16	1861–1865	Abraham Lincoln
17	1865–1869	Andrew Johnson
18	1869–1877	Ulysses Grant
19	1877–1881	Rutherford Hayes
20	1881	James Garfield
21	1881–1885	Chester Arthur
22	1885–1889	Grover Cleveland
23	1889–1893	Benjamin Harrison
24	1893–1897	Grover Cleveland
25	1897–1901	William McKinley
26	1901–1909	Theodore Roosevelt
27	1909–1913	William Taft
28	1913–1921	Woodrow Wilson
29	1921–1923	Warren Harding
30	1923–1929	Calvin Coolidge
31	1929–1933	Herbert Hoover
32	1933–1945	Franklin Roosevelt
33	1945–1953	Harry S. Truman
34	1953–1961	Dwight Eisenhower
35	1961–1963	John Kennedy
36	1963–1969	Lyndon Johnson
37	1969–1974	Richard Nixon
38	1974–1977	Gerald Ford
39	1977–1981	Jimmy Carter
40	1981–1989	Ronald Reagan
41	1989–1992	George Bush
42	1993–2001	Bill Clinton
43	2001–2009	George Walker Bush
44	2009–2017	Barack Obama
45	2017–2021	Donald Trump

1 星期的**字首一定要大寫**，前面**不能加 the**，介系詞要搭配 on 來使用。

- **Monday** 星期一
- **Tuesday** 星期二
- **Wednesday** 星期三
- **Thursday** 星期四
- **Friday** 星期五
- **Saturday** 星期六
- **Sunday** 星期日

Call me on ~~the~~ Friday.
星期五打電話給我。

2 月分的**字首一定要大寫**，前面**不能加 the**，介系詞要搭配 in 來使用。

- **January** 一月
- **February** 二月
- **March** 三月
- **April** 四月
- **May** 五月
- **June** 六月
- **July** 七月
- **August** 八月
- **September** 九月
- **October** 十月
- **November** 十一月
- **December** 十二月

Let's go in ~~the~~ January.
我們一月去吧。

3 **日期**必須使用**序數詞**，完整的日期寫法，英式英語和美式英語不同。

英式英語	美式英語
15th January, 2025	January 15th, 2025
15 January, 2025	January 15, 2025
15.1.2025	1-15-2025
15.1.25	1-15-25

4 **日期**的介系詞要用 on。

We leave on January 10th.
我們 1 月 10 號出發。

Meet me on December 31st at 11 p.m. so we can ring in the New Year together.
12 月 31 號的晚上 11 點來找我，我們可以一起跨年。

5 **年分**的介系詞要用 in。

- in 1992 在 1992 年
- in **2006** 在 2006 年

年分的唸法

❶ **年分**的唸法，1999 年以前的，會分成**前後兩部分**來唸。
  1. 1999 nineteen ninety-nine
  2. 1876 eighteen seventy-six
  3. 1702 seventeen oh two (oh = zero)

❷ **年分**的唸法，2000 年以後的，則會唸成「**兩千 + 尾數**」。
  1. 2001 two thousand one
  2. 2005 two thousand five
  3. 2010 two thousand ten
  4. 2012 two thousand twelve

❸ **日期**（幾月幾日）的唸法有兩種：

  1 月 4 日
  1. the fourth of January
  2. January (the) fourth

Practice

1

依據 **Mr. Simpson** 的一週行事曆，造句描述他每一天的行程。

1. Mr. Simpson is meeting Ms. Miller on Monday.

2. ....

....

3. ....

....

4. ....

....

5. ....

....

6. ....

....

7. ....

....

Appointment Book

Mon.

meet Mr. Miller

Tue.

visit his grandma

Wed.

go shopping

Thur.

have dinner with Tom

Fri.

pick up Peter at the airport

Sat.

play basketball

Sun.

go to the movies

2

用英文寫出右列日期的唸法。

1. 20. 5. 19

→ ....

2. 19. 6. 1996

→ ....

3. 1. 3. 2018

→ ....

4. 10-11-1502

→ ....

5. 2-26-2010

→ ....

6. 12-31-1876

→ ....

Part 14 Numbers, Time, and Dates
數字、時間和日期

Unit 105

Time of Day
時間

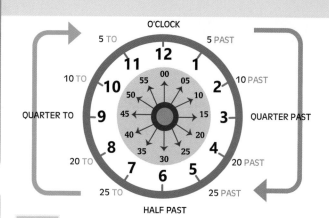

1 用 o'clock 來表示「**整點**」。

nine o'clock
9 a.m./9 p.m.
九點鐘

five o'clock
5 a.m./5 p.m.
五點鐘

2 用 half past 來表示「**幾點半**」。
（此為英式讀法）

half past **two**
兩點半

half past **one**
一點半

3 用 (a) quarter past 表「**幾點過 15 分**」；
用 (a) quarter to 表示「**差 15 分幾點**」。
（此為英式讀法）

a quarter past
twelve
十二點十五分

a quarter to
three
兩點四十五分

4 用 minutes past 表示「**幾點過幾
分**」；用 minutes to 表示「**差幾分
幾點**」。（此為英式讀法）

twenty-six
minutes past **seven**
七點二十六分

twenty-two
minutes to **ten**
九點三十八分

5 如果分鐘為 5 的倍數，就**省略
minutes**。（此為英式讀法）

five past **nine**
九點五分

ten past **ten**
十點十分

6 另一種說明時間的方法為
「hour（時）+ the minutes（分）」。
（此為美式讀法）

two oh **two**
兩點零二分

one fifty-**two**
一點五十二分

seven thirty
七點半

twelve eighteen
十二點十八分

Practice

1

依據圖示，自下表選出
正確的時間填空。
（下面皆為英式讀法）

- Ⓐ half past two
- Ⓑ ten past ten
- Ⓒ five to four
- Ⓓ five o'clock
- Ⓔ ten to twelve
- Ⓕ two minutes to twelve

 ① D
 ②
 ③
 ④
 ⑤
 ⑥

2

依據圖示，分別用兩
種方式，以完整句子
描述時間。

（第二題除外，第二
題只有一種寫法。）

 1 It's a quarter past nine.
It's nine fifteen.

 2

 3

 4

 5

 6

 7

1   在空格內填入正確的星期或月分。
→ Unit 104 重點複習

1. The Chinese New Year is always in _____ or _____.
2. Easter always falls on a _____.
3. _____ is the third month.
4. _____ is the eighth month.
5. Mother's Day is on the second _____ of May.
6. _____ comes after Wednesday.
7. _____ the 13th occurs when the 13th day of a month falls on a Friday.
8. In Taiwan, typhoons occur mostly in _____, _____, and _____.
9. Thanksgiving Day falls on the fourth _____ of _____.
10. People born from late _____ to early _____ are Geminis.

2   用「the . . . of . . .」的形式，在空格內填入正確的日期。
→ Unit 104 重點複習

1. Christmas Day is on _____.
2. New Year's Eve falls on _____.
3. New Year's Day falls on _____.
4. Valentine's Day is on _____.
5. The Dragon Boat Festival is on _____ of the Chinese lunar calendar.
6. The Chinese Valentine's Day falls on _____ of the Chinese lunar calendar.
7. The Autumn Festival is on _____ of the Chinese lunar calendar.
8. Halloween is celebrated on _____.
9. Is that true people born on _____ can only celebrate their birthday once every four years?

3 寫出下列各項資訊的唸法。
→ Unit 104 重點複習

電話號碼

1. 8930-7635

  → _____

2. 02-3478-9711

  → _____

3. 886-2-115-6730

  → _____

4. 4561-8932 Ext. 112

  → _____

5. 0965-321-578

  → _____

日期

6. 三月二十八日

  → _____

7. 七月四日

  → _____

8. 一月一日

  → _____

9. 九月十八日

  → _____

年分

10. 1459

  → _____

11. 1938

  → _____

12. 2009

  → _____

13. 2020

  → _____

Progress Test

1 將括弧內動詞以正確的形態填空，完成句子。

1. I can _____ (use) the computer.
2. I want _____ (use) the computer.
3. I like _____ (use) the computer.
4. We may _____ (finish) early.
5. Let's _____ (call) your cousin tonight.
6. I hope _____ (see) the museum soon.
7. Can you help _____ (stuff) the mailboxes?
8. It's too late _____ (start) now.
9. How about _____ (start) tomorrow?
10. Jane asked me _____ (send) her the contract as soon as possible.
11. Is it difficult _____ (learn) Japanese?
12. No, Japanese is easy _____ (learn) .
13. Are you good at _____ (play) video games?
14. Would you like me _____ (turn) on the lights?
15. Do you mind _____ (hold) the ladder for me while I change the light bulb?

2 請用 to 或 for 填空，完成句子。

1. He went to the store _____ some soy milk.
2. He wants soy milk _____ his breakfast cereal.
3. He went to the mini-mart _____ buy soy milk.
4. He drinks soy milk _____ stay healthy.

Part 7 常用動詞

1 請將括弧內的動詞以正確的形式填空，完成下列句子。

1. I'm going _____ (shop) with Elaine tomorrow. Would you like to join us?
2. I can't get the car _____ (start). The battery must be dead.
3. Don't worry. I'll get someone _____ (fix) the car right away.
4. You can't make him _____ (do) anything he doesn't like.
5. I'll have him _____ (deliver) the package to your office.
6. Please have these boxes _____ (mail).
7. It took me thirty minutes _____ (walk) to the hospital.

2 請圈選正確的答案。

1. John and Lily went for swimming / a swim last Saturday.
2. My parents are going on to travel / a trip to Finland next month.
3. I'm thinking about taking / making the job he offered.
4. The statue of the lion is made of / from stone.
5. The meatballs are made of / from beef.
6. Did you have / get fun in Madrid?
7. David will make / do the dishes and I'll make / do the laundry.
8. The music festival will take place / part in November.

Part 8   情態助動詞

1   請圈選正確的答案。

1. How many push-ups can / can't you do?

2. He can / cans drive his car with his eyes shut.

3. He can / can't always say something that makes everybody mad.

4. The director can / can't see you right now, because he is at a meeting.

5. Can you / Do you can please help me take out the garbage?

2   請將錯誤的句子打✗，並寫出正確的句子。若句子無誤，則在方框內打 ✓。

1. I could talk when I was one year old.
   ☐ ....

2. He can't swim but he loves taking baths.
   ☐ ....

3. If I can I would, but I can't so I won't.
   ☐ ....

4. He can climb up trees when he was young, but he couldn't get down.
   ☐ ....
   ....

5. If anybody who can do it, Bobby Brown is the guy for the job.
   ☐ ....
   ....

3   請將括弧內的動詞搭配 must 或 mustn't 填空，完成句子。

1. You .... (tell) them who you are or they will throw you in jail.

2. You .... (pay) your phone bill or they will cut off your service.

3. No, you .... (eat) cookies before dinner or you will spoil your appetite.

4. He .... (call) to apologize. He has to accept responsibility for what he did.

4   請自下表選出適當的動詞，搭配 should 或 shouldn't 填空，完成句子。

ask	make	see	leave

1. Judy: I'm spending too much money on long distance calls.
   Sam: You .... so many calls.

2. Judy: You have an appointment. Why are you still here?
   Sam: You're right. I .... immediately.

3. Judy: I feel sick. Do I have a temperature?
   Sam: You have a fever. You .... a doctor.

4. Judy: Why is my bonus so small? I sold more cars than anybody else.
   Sam: Do you think you .... about how your bonus was awarded?

5 請用 must、have to、has to 或 had to 填空，完成下列句子。

1. You _____ drive at or less than the speed limit.

2. You _____ try the hot pot at this restaurant.

3. The dog _____ go to the bathroom.

4. My father _____ walk 5 km to work every day.

5. Did you _____ change all the estimates in the proposal?

6. You _____ finish by 5:00 or else you will end up working late.

6 請將下列單字重組為正確的句子。

1. in my account / the balance / check / can / you / ?
   → *Can you check the balance in my account?*

2. transfer / I / could / please / $20,000?
   → _____

3. an electronic fund transfer / the charges / you / could / go over / for / ?
   → _____

4. I / to fill out / this form / your pen / use / may / ?
   → _____

5. of / have / may / I / some extra copies / this EFT form / ?
   → _____

6. you / me / the baby / a bath / to give / like / would / ?
   → _____

7. the baby / while / to take / you / would / like / a break / I watch / ?
   → _____

8. for you / change / I'll / the baby's diaper / .
   → _____

9. I / some milk / your baby / for / warm up / should / ?
   → _____

10. for / I / a nap / put the baby / should / down / ?
    → _____

7 請用 shall、let's、why don't we 和 how about 填空，完成下列對話。

Max: The babysitter has finally arrived.

❶_____ leave right now.

Faye: ❷_____ go over a few details with her first?

Max: She's a babysitter. She knows how to take care of kids. What ❸_____ we do tonight?

Faye: ❹_____ telling the babysitter where we are going?

Max: Fine. Where ❺_____ we go?

Faye: I don't know. Maybe we should go to see my mother.

Max: ❻_____ I go to a movie with my friend, Wolfman?

Faye: OK. I'm coming. ❼_____ leave now?

Part 9　句子類型

1 自下表選出適當的疑問詞填空，完成下列問答。

what	why	which	whose	how
when	who	where	how old	how often

1. Q _____ is your boss?
   A His name is Peter.

2. Q _____ is your job?
   A English Teacher.

3. Q _____ do you like more, books or movies?
   A Books.

4. Q _____ coat is this?
   A It's Albert's coat.

5. Q _____ is your car?
   A In the school parking lot.

6. Q _____ do you eat breakfast?
   A At 5:30 a.m.

7. Q _____ do you eat so early?
   A I have a long commute.

8. Q _____ do you get to work?
   A I drive on the highway.

9. Q _____ are your children?
   A They are 5 and 7 years old.

10. Q _____ do you see a dentist?
    A Never. I am afraid of dentists.

2 請依據題意，寫出問句完成下列問答。

1. Q *What are you doing?*

   A I'm watching a movie.

2. Q _____

   A The movie is about a man trying to save his daughter.

3. Q _____

   A The daughter was kidnapped.

4. Q _____

   A The man rescues his daughter at the end of the movie .

3 請填上正確的附加問句。

1. You're happy, _____?
2. It's late, _____?
3. Tom can't go, _____?
4. I'm not very tall, _____?
5. You have three aces, _____?
6. Frank won the game, _____?

4 自下表選出適當的動詞或片語填空，完成下列祈使句。

pass	not forget	not take	sit
come	move		call

1. _____ your mother right now.
2. _____ that ladder before getting the box.
3. Please _____ in and _____ down.
4. _____ the last piece.
5. _____ to write the financial report.
6. Please _____ me the peas and potatoes.

1 請選出正確的答案。

_____ 1. Everyone ran out of the building when the fire alarm _____.
   Ⓐ went on
   Ⓑ went off
   Ⓒ took off

_____ 2. Can you _____ your father and mother in-law?
   Ⓐ get over with
   Ⓑ get away with
   Ⓒ get along with

_____ 3. I feel like _____. Can I have an airsickness bag?
   Ⓐ throwing up
   Ⓑ throwing away
   Ⓒ throwing off

_____ 4. _____ the volume or you'll wake up the kids.
   Ⓐ Turn down
   Ⓑ Turn around
   Ⓒ Turn on

_____ 5. They _____ the trip to Korea because their grandma was sick.
   Ⓐ called on
   Ⓑ called off
   Ⓒ called in

_____ 6. Winnie _____ a proposal at the conference last Thursday.
   Ⓐ brought in
   Ⓑ brought up
   Ⓒ brought about

7. He's _____ his promise to stop playing video games on weekdays.
   Ⓐ carried out
   Ⓑ carried away
   Ⓒ carried on

8. The police tried to _____ more information about the murder victim.
   Ⓐ find out
   Ⓑ find for
   Ⓒ find about

2 請用正確的介系詞填空，完成句子。

1. The remote control airplane belongs _____ Johnny.
2. Keep away _____ the stove.
3. I'm looking forward _____ seeing you again.
4. Watch out _____ the falling rocks.
5. How can you put up _____ a man who never takes a shower?
6. Why are you searching the room? What are you looking _____?

>>> **Part 11** 形容詞和副詞

1 請圈選正確的答案。

1. This milk tea is too sweet / enough sweet.
2. The music isn't loud enough / enough loud.
3. Her attitude is too bitter / enough bitter for me.
4. Even decaf coffee is too / very tasty to drink.

2 將錯誤的句子打✗，並寫出正確的句子。若句子無誤，則打✓。

1. That's a cool computer.
   ☐ _____

2. It's a computer fast.
   ☐ _____

3. The screen is bright.
   ☐ _____

4. The machine light is.
   ☐ _____

3 將下列詞彙與片語重組，以正確語序完成句子，並在結尾加上正確的標點符號。

1. leave / I / at 10:00
   → *I leave at 10:00.* _____

2. at my house / pick me up / at 7:00
   → _____

3. always / to go dancing / dresses up / Greg
   → _____

4. to arrive / the first / never / Teddy / is
   → _____

5. were playing / the kids / yesterday / at the park
   → _____

6. she / five minutes ago / ran to the car / quickly
   → _____

4 寫出下列形容詞的「比較級」和「最高級」。

1. nice ....
2. small ....
3. sad ....
4. busy ....
5. pretty ....
6. good ....
7. bad ....
8. much ....
9. important

....
....

10. popular

....
....

11. successful

....
....

12. boring

....
....

5 請圈選正確的答案。

1. He is a little too smooth / smoothly.
2. Spread the frosting smooth / smoothly.
3. It was an awfully / awful performance.
4. He is so earnest / earnestly it makes me gag.
5. It was incredible / incredibly boring if you ask me.
6. I'd say they were artificial / artificially enhanced.

6 請圈選正確的答案。

I'm a couch potato. I love watching TV and eating snacks. Guess how I rank walking, running, and exercising.

1. A little bit of walking is bad / worse / worst.
2. Running and sweating is bad / worse / worst.
3. Heart pounding exercise like sit-ups and push-ups are the bad / worse / worst.

Some people like tight clothes. Guess how tight these are.

4. Those pants are as tight / tighter / tightest as a pair of socks, but they look good.
5. That shirt is tight / tighter / tightest than a swimsuit, and it shows everything.
6. Why are you wearing the tight / tighter / tightest possible clothing? It looks incredibly uncomfortable.
7. He doesn't look like an important / more important / most important guy with those old wrinkled clothes.
8. He is wearing a nice suit, and he looks important / more important / most important than most of the other managers here.
9. Wow. That guy is being followed by secret service agents. He looks like the important / more important / most important guy to arrive here.

Part 12   介系詞

1   請用 **in**、**on** 或 **at** 填空，完成句子。

1. Your earrings are _____ the table _____ the blue dish.

2. We live _____ the No. 12 bus line near the last stop.

3. He may be _____ work or _____ home, but I haven't seen him.

4. She is _____ school _____ the biochemistry building.

5. His flight was delayed, so he waited _____ the gift shop _____ the airport.

6. He used to live _____ 323 Hamilton Street _____ Evansville.

2   請用 **in**、**on** 或 **at** 填空，完成句子，若不需要使用介系詞，則畫✗。

1. From Monday through Friday I get up _____ 5 a.m. and go to bed _____ 9 p.m.

2. On the weekends I often take naps _____ the afternoon and go out _____ night.

3. My daughter was born _____ June 1st, 1991.

4. I like to take long walks _____ the weekends _____ the summer.

5. I'm not too busy _____ this weekend, so maybe we can meet _____ tomorrow morning.

3   請圈選正確的答案。

1. I parked my car near / in my apartment in front of / on a fire hydrant.

2. The pet store is next to / onto a Thai restaurant and down / opposite the Mayflower Department Store.

3. I slipped up / into this bad mood, and I can't get out of / under it.

4. When the tide was low, I walked from / to an island. Now the tide is high and I can't get off / between the island.

5. When I want exercise, I take the elevator past / up to the top floor, and then I walk down / round to the ground floor.

6. I have a short cut to my office, through / under an alley and off / across a parking lot.

7. The road goes over / between the highway and on / under the train tracks.

8. Walk past / through the old lady selling flowers and onto / around the breakfast vendor, and it's between / in the bus stop and the corner.

9. I went to / up the night market with lots of money, and on my way home between / from the market I realized I had spent it all.

4   將錯誤的句子打✗，並用 **for**、**since** 或 **ago** 改寫出正確的句子。若句子無誤，則在方框內打✓。

1. They left for lunch an hour since.
   □ _They left for lunch an hour ago._

2. I graduated ten years ago.
   □ _____

3. We have been working on the report since 1:00.

☐ ....

....

4. I have been shopping since an hour.

☐ ....

5. I have been reading the newspaper for one hour.

☐ ....

....

6. The package has been here since Tuesday.

☐ ....

....

▶▶▶ Part 13 連接詞

1 請用 when 或 if 填空，完成句子。

1. I'll have to get used to the crying .... my mom brings my baby brother home.

2. I want a wedding in Spain .... I get married to Pablo.

3. I will buy a new house .... I win the lottery.

4. .... I graduate from barber school, I want to get a job cutting hair in the mall.

5. .... I get up tomorrow, I am going to make my husband cook breakfast.

6. .... my wife finds out, then I'm in big trouble.

2 請圈選正確的答案。

1. Those three people are Yuki, Kuan, and / or Sayed.

2. Would you like fish so / and chips?

3. I don't like fried fish, but / and I'll take an order of chips.

4. Are you single or / because married?

5. I am single or / because I can't find a wife.

6. I am married because / so I don't go to singles bars.

3 請用 because 或 so 填空，完成句子。

1. Yesterday I bought a present for my mother .... it was her birthday.

2. I put the package in the back seat of my car, ... I could take it to her house.

3. My mom was happy .... I remembered her birthday.

4. I offered to take her out to dinner .... I don't know how to cook.

5. I didn't tell her we were going to her sister's house, ... her party would be a surprise.

6. She suspected something .... she recognized several cars outside her sister's house.

7. I told her I had to pick up a gift, ... it would sound sort of reasonable.

8. The house looked empty when we walked in .... everybody was hiding.

9. Everybody waited a while before shouting surprise, ... she would be surprised.

10. My mom was really surprised .... waiting for two minutes really fooled her into thinking there was no party.

>>> **Part 14　數字、時間和日期**

1　寫出下列數字、日期或時間的唸法。

1. 34 ....

2. 143 ....

3. 1895 ....

4. 8000 ....

5. (03) 3459-8431

....

6. 9th and 10th ....

7. April 20th ....

8. 8:00 ....

9. 8:30 ....

10. 8:08 ....

11. 8:45 ....

2　填空完成句子。

1. The first two days of the week are
.... and ....

2. The first and second months of the year
are .... and ....

3. Saturday and Sunday are called the
....

4. The season that comes after summer is
....

5. Most people start working .... the
morning and go to bed .... night.

Let's See Grammar

Basic 2

彩圖初級英文文法　三版

作　　　者	Alex Rath Ph.D.
審　　　訂	Dennis Le Boeuf & Liming Jing
譯　　　者	謝右／丁宥榆
校　　　對	歐寶妮
編　　　輯	賴祖兒／丁宥榆／陸葵珍
主　　　編	丁宥暄
內 文 設 計	洪伊珊／林書玉
封 面 設 計	林書玉
圖 片 協 力	周演音
製 程 管 理	洪巧玲
出　版　者	寂天文化事業股份有限公司
發　行　人	周均亮
電　　　話	+886-(0)2-2365-9739
傳　　　真	+886-(0)2-2365-9835
網　　　址	www.icosmos.com.tw
讀 者 服 務	onlineservice@icosmos.com.tw
出 版 日 期	2021 年 2 月 三版一刷

國家圖書館出版品預行編目 (CIP) 資料

Let's See Grammar：彩圖初級英文文法 Basic / Alex
Rath 著 . -- 三版 . -- [臺北市]：寂天文化事業股份有限
公司 , 2021.02
面；　公分
ISBN 978-986-318-973-2　（第 1 冊：菊 8K 平裝）
ISBN 978-986-318-974-9　（第 2 冊：菊 8K 平裝）
1. 英語　2. 語法
805.16　　　　　　　　　　　　　110000944